The
Bennington
Stitch

The Bennington Stitch

Sheila Solomon Klass

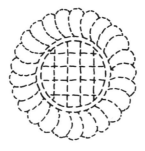

CHARLES SCRIBNER'S SONS
NEW YORK

Copyright © 1985 Sheila Solomon Klass

Library of Congress Cataloging in Publication Data
Klass, Sheila Solomon.   The Bennington stitch.
Summary: As a young girl, Amy's mother had been
denied the chance to attend Bennington College and
now is determined that seventeen-year-old Amy will
have that opportunity whether she wants it or not.
[1. Mothers and daughters—Fiction]   I. Title.
PZ7.K67814Be   1985   [Fic]   85-40291
ISBN 0-684-18436-2

1 3 5 7 9 11 13 15 17 19   F/C   20 18 16 14 12 10 8 6 4 2

Printed in the United States of America

For Benjamin
—wonderfully promising,
promising wonders

The
Bennington
Stitch

1

I was coming down the stairs at three-thirty, one bitter late January afternoon, when I ran into Mr. O'Brien—Mr. O to seniors—our college guidance counselor. "All right, Amy," he said, pointing a forefinger at me and transfixing me there.

I waited. Mr. O is a movie buff who founded our school Cinema Club and is its faculty adviser. He's an encyclopedia of film information, a little nutty on the subject of the movies as the greatest twentieth century art form.

> " 'There's a cyclops,'
> 'But he's got two eyes,'
> 'A bicyclops.' "

I knew the lines but I couldn't place them fast enough. "You've got me."

"*Yellow Submarine.*"

"Of course."

"I thought you'd know it, Amy, because we showed it here last year. Care to try one more?"

I nodded.

" 'We must be doing something right to last two hundred years.' "

"Ah ha," I said triumphantly. "*Nashville.*"

Mr. O smiled his big hearty smile at me. He's a large, heavy, white-haired polar bear of a man. Mom says his hair has been white since he was thirty. "Good guess," he said. "Now for the real world. SAT scores are coming this week."

Bad news.

"You'll want to see me. You know where my office is. Don't be shy." Before I had a chance to fall apart, he asked, "Want to try me on one?"

"Yes," I said. "I've been saving one for you. 'Follow the money.' "

He drew back a step, pretending to be hurt. "I'm disappointed in your low opinion of me. That's Deep Throat talking in *All the President's Men.*"

"Does anyone ever stump you, Mr. O?"

"Your mother did this afternoon in the faculty lunchroom. Ruined my lunch."

"My mother? With what line?"

" 'You found paradise in America.' "

That drew a blank from me.

"I was suffering a temporary memory lapse brought on by the terrible tuna fish salad," he said, "because I know that line is from *The Godfather.* Brando says it at the beginning to a wedding guest."

I clasped my hands together and raised them over my head. "Yay, Mom!"

"Tell your mother it was an aberration. And when the scores come from the Educational Testing Service, remember"—his blue eyes got that glazed look that means Movie-Quote-to-Follow—" 'I'll be right here.' "

"*E.T.*," I said.

He waved and was gone.

My scores on the PSATs taken last year when I was a junior were pathetic. I hoped I would do a little better on the senior exams. Everyone takes them and tries their best and knows everyone else's results; it's the twelfth grade marathon. It was my mother's fantasy, however, that I would do *much much* better on these new tests. In fact, she convinced herself that these scores will wipe away the old ones.

My mother cannot accept the reality of her daughter: me.

I walked home as slowly as possible. When doom is about to descend you cannot escape it; I knew that. I was merely trying to delay it.

3

2

"Hi, Amy. Got a little something for you here," our mailman said, handing over the mail. I reached for the packet of letters, and, recognizing the squarish blue-trimmed envelope on top, postmarked Princeton, New Jersey, I felt suddenly as if I'd been punched in the belly. Hard. A knockout blow.

Belly? Mom would frown. *Stomach, abdomen, solar plexus, middle.* If she took the college entrance exams, she'd get eight hundreds. She writes like an angel, and she's a whiz at whatever she chooses to study. She loves words in any language. She taught herself German last year. And botany. Go for a walk with her and she identifies every growing plant. Even weeds.

"You couldn't send this letter back marked 'Addressee Unknown,' or 'Gone to Gondwanaland,' or something, could you?"

"Where's that? Gondwanaland?" The mailman looked suspicious. "Been working for the U.S. Postal Service for twenty-nine years, and I never heard—"

"Oh, it's just a joke. Millions of years ago, Gondwanaland was the part of the world that is now Africa and South America. It was all joined together once, and then later it broke apart."

He scratched his earlobe. He could have been a twin to that farmer in the painting *American Gothic*: skinny, stern-faced, wire-rimmed specs. "Smart girl like you knows about Gondwanaland has nothing to worry about in *that* envelope." He pointed with his chin to the blue-trimmed death sentence in that stack of mail.

"Naah. I know lots of junk, but none of it is worth much. My middle name is Trivia." I realized at once that I had made a terrible mistake. Because he delivered our mail, he knew! Sure enough, he began to chuckle.

"I thought your middle name was Bloomer." The chuckle turned into a cough, and it took him a minute to stop. "Pretty remarkable name, that."

"You're right," I said bitterly. "I'm the only girl on earth who would be better off with Trivia for a middle name."

"You'll be fine, Amy. You'll go to college with the best of them."

"You've put your finger right on the problem," I mumbled.

His weatherbeaten face looked intensely sincere as he leaned back and prepared to go on talking. He took no notice of the cold. This is one mailman who never heard of the Postal Service motto: *Neither snow, nor rain, nor heat,*

5

nor gloom of night stays these couriers from the swift com-
pletion of their appointed rounds. Gossip stays *him* every
time. The rest of the folks on his route can just whistle for
their mail once he gets to talking.

"Sorry, I have to go in now and get dinner started for
Mom," I said hurriedly, anticipating his monologue. *You
kids with your problems. You got everythin' and you're still
not happy. Everythin'. When I was your age I was walkin'
around with cardboard in my shoes for soles. Cardboard! And
I still wasn't complainin'! A lot of good it would've done me,
eh?* . . . I had heard him on the subject of his cardboard soles
many times. I just wasn't up to cardboard today.

He nodded, looking perplexed and a little disappointed;
then he slung his bag higher on his shoulder and went on his
way. I turned up the front walk and slowly went inside.

I carried in the mail and put it on the mantel without
opening my letter. If I could have, I would have carried it
right out back to the trash can in the yard. But I couldn't.

I headed for the kitchen, ready to try an eighteenth-
century version of Yankee Pot Roast for which I had stocked
up on most of the ingredients days before. Just now I'd
stopped off at Colonial Cookery, and Jessie Campbell, who
had unearthed this recipe (and who last week had taught me
how to make sensational scones), provided the secret in-
gredient: a handful of dried currants. Some normal Yankee
housewife had had a poetic impulse one day long ago: currants in with the carrots, potatoes, turnips, and onions. Wild!

Jessie is a culinary authority. She moved here last summer
after her marriage broke up, and she supports herself and her

6

daughter Jan, my classmate, with the store, a sort of offbeat grocery and bakery, and with a part-time job teaching Home Economics in our high school. She advises the Homemakers Club, my major extracurricular activity. I'm president this year. Jessie is writing a cookbook of early New England recipes to be called *The Yankee Doodle Cookbook.* She often tests recipes on Jan and me. I'm the world expert on New England pies: rhubarb, cranberry, blackberry, buttermilk. Those colonists could fight and those colonists could bake!

I was glad I had stopped and picked up the currants so I could try the pot roast. I wanted to do something complicated that would engross me. Something, anything that would push back/keep away the inevitable scene with my mother set for later that evening.

Inside that square blue-trimmed envelope was a series of numbers that added up to a broken promise. I felt terrible about it even though it was a foolish promise and not one that I, myself, had made.

3

Seconds after I was born, my intellectual mother, who had been given only a spinal anesthetic and therefore claims that her mind was perfectly clear, made a solemn twofold vow: "This child will be called Amelia Bloomer Hamilton, and she will study the arts at Bennington College. Nothing will prevent this!"

It was a favorite family story; I heard it from my mother, from my uncle George, and from Dr. Burton, still our family doctor, who says he was working away sewing my mother up, while a nurse held me in my newborn, slippery, messy state, when suddenly my mother uttered this startling pledge, nearly causing him to drop a stitch and the nurse to drop me. Dr. Burton, who is rather conservative and cares a lot about professional dignity, has never quite forgiven Mom for that delivery room behavior.

I let out my first cry then, good and loud, without need of any slap on the bottom. My mother remembers this first cry fondly, "as a sort of college cheer, though of course Bennington is not that kind of a college." I look upon it as our first disagreement.

I had good reason to yell. My fate was sealed in that sentence. I am doomed to keep that name, at least till I come of age. And I am doomed to disappoint my mother.

When there are two parents around, maybe they think more about each other, and that takes the pressure off the kid. But my father is dead. He died when I was two, when his motorbike skidded off the road into a ditch. All I remember of him is he was big and kind and he smiled a lot. Maybe I don't even remember; maybe it's all the pictures we have of him around the house. In them he's big and kind and smiling.

Take my name as an example of parents' extreme lack of consideration. Amelia *Bloomer* Hamilton. Even after kids stop snickering at it, and they like me enough to consider the matter seriously, it is hard for them to believe that in the 1960s, when the Beatles were singing, and Dr. Martin Luther King, Jr. was preaching, and JFK was president and then was assassinated, and there were all kinds of civil rights movements, American parents—educated intelligent people— would do that to a baby who didn't do anything to them except get born. Well, Thomas and Doris Hamilton did it.

"How could you do such a terrible thing to me?" I asked Mom repeatedly. "Amelia *Bloomer* Hamilton. How would you like to be Doris *Snuggies* Hamilton? Doris *Hip-huggers* Hamilton? Doris *Bikini* Hamilton?"

"*Drawers*—" My mother chuckled. "You forgot drawers. Amy, I've explained all of this to you before. Daddy and I chose your name when we were courting."

9

"Courting?" I tried not to smirk. It is wild having a mother who is an English teacher. You never know what century she talketh in.

"Yes," she said. "Daddy and I agreed that when we were married, if we had a son we would call him Edgar Allan. Daddy had just started writing his thesis on Poe, and he was deep into his writing."

"How come you didn't decide to call the kid Raven? Or me Ulalume?" Mom used to read Poe's stories and poems to me. It was a way of sharing something Daddy had loved. "Or Lady Usher? Madeline Usher Hamilton." I tried it out and shuddered. Lady Usher rose from the dead in Poe's mad story. She was no one to be named after, and no one to make jokes about.

"Well," Mom said lightly, "look at it this way; if you were an Usher you might find part-time work in—"

"A movie house or a summer theater," I finished her sentence with her, both of us giggling.

"You know," my mother went on, "I am distantly related to Amelia Bloomer, on my mother's side, and I've always admired her, though secretly, because my father would not allow mention of her name in our house."

"I don't blame him. Bloomer is a gross name." I had interrupted, but nothing really interrupts Mother. In fact, that's true of all teachers.

"She was incredible. In the 1800s, when women were all wearing long, clumsy skirts, she started wearing short skirts with loose trousers buttoned at the ankles: the forerunners of jeans. And slacks. We owe Amelia Bloomer for our freedom of dress. She is my idea of a worthy model."

"I hate that word, *model.*"

"How can you hate a word, Amy?"

"I hate it. Who needs one from real life? There are plenty of wonderful made-up ones: Jo March, Scarlett O'Hara, Cathy Earnshaw, Princess Leia."

"Who?"

"Princess Leia. You remember—in *Star Wars?*"

Mom laughed and turned to other things, the way she does when I'm too much for her. She simply doesn't understand me. She teaches high school here in Eastfield, and, though it is carefully arranged that I am never in her classes, I am Amelia Bloomer Hamilton and I cannot escape her shadow.

She would like to arrange my life for me every bit as much as mothers in faraway places like Iran and India do for their daughters. She still tries to tell me what to eat and what to wear. Every time it rains she tells me to put on my boots. *Every single time!* She has the best intentions. The terrible thing about all of this is that the best-intentioned parents can ruin their children's lives that way, and there is very little the children can do about it. Even in the land of the free and the home of the brave.

My name doesn't sound anything like me. I'm small, ninety-five pounds; petite, resembling my mother. I have long, straight, tar-black hair (hers is graying now), very pale skin with a few freckles, and emerald-green eyes. I am a size six, which does not sound one bit like Amelia Bloomer Hamilton, or even Amy. That's a sharp, clumsy, raw-boned name. I like names like Chrissy, Bianca, Jodie, or Jane.

I know what to do about my name. I'll change it, of course, as soon as I'm of age. I might keep the Hamilton, but everything else goes. Fast. I haven't chosen my new name yet, but I spend a lot of time going over the possibilities. I just want a pretty name. Even if I do something remarkable with my life, I hope babies won't be named after me. I don't want to put that monkey on anyone else's back. Not me. I am definitely a type: a Bianca person, a Jodie, a Chrissy, or a Jane. Since I have years before I can legally make the change, I have plenty of time to review new names.

I do that a lot. I sit and listen to records, and I study name lists published for parents-to-be. They're very interesting. Many names have special meanings. Bianca means white. Chrissy is a form of Christian. Jane means God is generous. (That's a lovely one.) Jodie means praised. Guess what Amelia means? *Industrious*. I suppose that one was obvious.

I cook a lot because I like to and because my mother is often up in the attic, writing. She writes short stories and poems, but she doesn't like to show them to anyone. She says she's waiting until they're good enough. "You might be old or dead by then," I say, but she only shrugs. She's been working on a novel for years and years. I think she used to show her work to my father, and once in a while she'll try a short piece out on Mr. O, or on me, but no one has ever seen or heard so much as a line of her novel.

She also works hard at school, running the literary magazine, *Pen & Ink*. Nobody writes in pen anymore when they submit stuff; they type or they use word processors. But she won't consider changing the magazine's name. Anyway, *Pen & Ink* is her extracurricular activity. She hates to cook. Hates it! But, to be fair, she never puts it off on me. If it were up to her we'd eat takeout chicken nightly. I choose to cook. Sometimes I think it bothers her that I do, but that's crazy. I'm sure she's glad to get a good meal in the evening.

Lets' face it—I have many problems, but the biggest one is a Mother Problem. Part of the trouble is that I am all she has. I was born after many years of waiting, when they had almost given up hope of having a child. Mother had a difficult pregnancy, complications, and finally, a Cesarean section. For my parents, my birth was a kind of minor miracle. I, Amelia Bloomer Hamilton, seem to be the last of the line. Uncle George is a bachelor, but all the women he goes out with look emaciated: eye shadow and cheekbones and skinny skinny bodies. I doubt that any of them would want—or could have —kids.

I suppose since I am the last of the line, I should have turned out better. I'm a disappointment to Mother. College-educated parents, particularly if they're teachers, believe that liberal arts degrees and breathing are equally essential for life.

One thing I do know: it is hard to teach a teacher— anything.

13

4

If the first half of my mother's birthing vow was inconvenient for me, the second half was disaster!

I've heard of people who decide when their babies are born that the kids will grow up to attend their alma mater. They love the old school so much they want their children to share that love. But my mother never *went* to Bennington. She had hoped to go, to learn to write poetry and fiction. Her high school teachers said she had talent. I've seen the comments on her papers. (She still has them.) But Mother's hopes were wildly unrealistic. Her father, a minister, had fixed ideas on the subject of women and education. Of course, he said *no*.

He sent her brother George to Brown, where Georgie Porgie (his undergraduate nickname because, he says, he majored in kissing girls from neighboring schools) took five strenuous athletic years to complete his A.B. He went on into publishing, where he earns lots of money and seems to me to be having a good time. I am very fond of Uncle George.

My mother, at eighteen, using all the energy and courage and persuasiveness she could muster, got herself sent to a small state college that trained teachers. Grandfather was even reluctant to do that much. He believed women should be docile and domestic.

I've been over all this a million times before with Rob, my boyfriend. He and I go all the way back to infancy as friends. It was his father, Dr. Burton, who nearly dropped the Bennington stitch at my birth. Rob, one day, will look just like his father; he's six feet tall, bony-faced, Lincolnesque. He has strong features: brown hair that stands up as if it's electrified, and brown shaggy eyebrows, intense dark piercing eyes behind horn-rimmed glasses, beautiful, even teeth. He's interested in people and he listens. He's also enormously talented as an artist. He can draw anything: landscapes, portraits, figures, even cartoons. What he'd like to do most in this world is study art in Paris and Florence.

But no go. His father has visions of Rob in white coat and stethoscope, joining his practice. Dr. Burton is a terrific doctor; he can make a correct diagnosis at ten paces. But he's a tough, unbending father. He lost his elder son, Pete, to professional baseball four years ago. Pete just packed up and went to Florida, where he plays ball now. He, too, was programmed for medicine. Rob's mother sides with art and baseball against medicine, but mostly she plays bridge and stays out of it.

Maybe the reason Rob and I are so close is because we share a common agony—we each have one parent dying to be a model.

Dr. Burton wants Rob to grow up to be what he *is*; my mother wants me to grow up to be what she *wanted to be*. I can't say which is worse.

After months of battling it out at home and then spending two hours in a rowdy college conference with his father and Mr. O, who tried to arbitrate, Rob spent most of his Christmas vacation doing college applications. His father had insisted on Yale, absolutely; Rob himself had decided to apply to the State University of New York at Purchase, and Mr. O recommended the University of Connecticut as a backup school. So Rob spent the holiday writing essays about himself and making lists of his extracurricular activities and of all the courses he took. My friend Jan applied to four schools in the Boston area, where her father lives, so she could be a day student and save room and board. Most of the other seniors spent Christmas holiday that way. But not me.

Mr. O did his best to talk Mom into letting me apply to local community colleges, or to Marlboro or Wells or other small schools. She wouldn't budge. "Let Amy enjoy Christmas," she said. "She'll go to Bennington. You know they have a much later application deadline."

He cornered me privately later. "Amy, there's no guarantee that Bennington will accept you. Your mother, who is otherwise pretty normal, is way out on this subject. Always has been. She has this *idée fixe*, this obsession about you and college. But you ought to know that you might not have a school to go to in the fall. I believe in plenty of backups."

16

"That's all right, Mr. O," I said. "I don't mind."

He looked at me, puzzled. "Oh well, you can always start as a walk-in part-time student in any one of a number of schools, and later become a matriculant. It's irregular, but so is this whole situation."

I shrugged.

"If there ever was a person who is neither docile nor domestic, it's my mother," I told Rob. "She hates cooking; she hates cleaning. She worships 'the life of the mind'; almost nothing else counts for her."

"Why'd she get married and have a kid?"

"She fell in love with my father, and she wanted children. She just doesn't appreciate mindless work."

"I'm with her there," Rob said, "but it's got to be done."

"Yeah. And she'll even do it, but slapdash, fast. Without glorifying it. Her idea of a sensational cooking job is to do a three-minute egg in two minutes. You know, without the whole *homemaker* bit. Call her a homemaker, she'll sock you."

"You know, Amy," Rob said, laughing, "you exaggerate."

"No, I don't. I have a lot of trouble dealing with my mother, but I'd never say she doesn't have cause for being the way she is. Do you know that whenever my grandfather saw her reading he used to lift the book from her hands and send her into her mother's garden to cut flowers or to weed? 'The Good Book is the best book for young ladies,' he would say. If anyone gives her a plant these days—remember her class chipped in and gave her a poinsettia at Christmas?—

she prays it will die a quick and painless death so she won't be saddled with taking care of it."

"What happened to the poinsettia?"

"*Il est mort.*"

"*Dieu lui donne le repos!*" Rob held his hands palm-to-palm in prayer position, but he was grinning.

If Lincoln had only had a grin like Rob's, the Civil War might have been averted. He could have charmed the South into manumission. *Manumission: to release from slavery or servitude.* Boy, did I memorize words for those exams. And then I faced the printed page, and, as always in such situations, my mind was a *tabula rasa*: a clean slate. A blank.

I am examophobic.

Since first grade I have never been able to take written tests if other people are around. Never. I begin to feel that they're all watching me and judging me. I start to sweat and feel nauseous. Twice I've actually fainted. Whatever I've studied disappears from my mind. The whole experience is agony. Of course, when this was discovered about me, Mom took me for all kinds of medical examinations. When they couldn't find anything wrong, she had to resort to a shrink who talked to me about myself, endlessly. I was supposed to talk to him, but I hated the idea of turning myself inside out for this stranger. I didn't know him and I didn't like him. He wore sideburns like a bad guy in a Western. After a while, I just wouldn't go back to see him. So our school, which has provisions for "exceptional children" (that means everyone with serious problems), allows me to go along the regular college prep track; I get private oral exams or take-home tests.

Actually, I love to write and I can write well, but by myself in my room with the door locked. (Some of my writing gets into *Pen & Ink*, chosen by the *editors*, not by my prejudiced mother.) Mom has her attic; I have my room. I can understand her better than she understands me. To be fair, she functions well outside her attic; I *need* my room. Even my IQ test had to be done specially. Mom says I have a high IQ. They don't tell a person her own IQ because they have some kind of theory that it's not good for you to know. If I really do have a high IQ you could never tell it by my schoolwork. Mom reminds me regularly that many geniuses were erratic students. I'm no genius; what I am is an erratic student.

"I wonder," Rob said, "if your mother would have been this way if your grandfather had not been so dogmatic."

"Who knows? He died before I was born, which is just as well because he and I wouldn't have gotten on. He's probably the reason Mother behaves the way she does, but I have to live with her that way. In *her* head I'm already in school in southern Vermont. We've visited Bennington three times now. It's a lovely campus, and I know it's a wonderful, innovative, creative school. But I never for one minute considered going there."

"What've you got against the place?"

"Nothing. But you better than anyone else should understand. I'm not my mother. That's her dream, not mine."

19

"A common case of mistaken identity," Rob said ruefully.
"I feel like it's fatal."
"Only if you die from it. Here comes artificial respiration."
He hugged me and hugged me until I was comforted.

5

If my scores were here, then Rob must have his too. He wouldn't leave the envelope unopened, not Rob. He's one of those life-confronters, one of those grab-the-problem-by-the-ears-and-shake-it-and-teach-it-who's-boss boys.

It was only a matter of minutes. I was slicing the four onions the recipe called for into thick slices, and weeping onion tears—good excuse—when the phone rang.

"Amy? They're here. My scores."

"How'd you do?"

"English: 750; math: 780."

"Fantastic scores, Rob."

" 'Tweren't nothin'."

"Congratulations on nothing, then."

"In a way, that's the case, Amy. You know now I'm in deep trouble."

"I know."

"It's just like some big crazy joke. I don't know what I'll do," he said. "I just don't know."

He was in as much trouble with his high scores as I was going to be with my low ones. I didn't have any advice for him.

"Scores like mine are perfect for the elite liberal arts undergraduate college—meaning Yale—leading right on to the elite medical school. My father will point all this out to me—again. 'Three generations of Burtons have excelled in science at Yale, Robert . . .'"

"Rob, I don't know what to tell you. High scores also get you into first-class art programs."

"Of course. If I could just convince Dad that every artist does not go mad and cut off his ear. And that I am not doctor material."

"It's going to be harder because of your brother," I said. "If Pete hadn't—"

His voice surged with pride over the telephone. "But Pete did it. Pete had guts and he's doing what he wanted to do, and he's doing it so well!"

"What'll you do, Rob?"

"I'll have to think of something. Never mind me. The mailman said he gave you your letter, too, Amy. Said it was a shame you didn't open it, so's he could tell me how you did."

"He hung around here waiting."

"You would've made his day. He lives through all of us through our mail."

"I know. But today I was feeling selfish. I wanted to keep it private."

"How'd you do, Amy?"

"I don't know. I didn't open the letter. I'm not going to. I figure Mom cares the most about what I got. Let her open it."

"Oh, come on, Amy. They're your scores. You open the letter."

"No, Rob. I'll wait. I can't talk anymore now. I'm cooking." I could barely manage a whisper. "See you." I hung up.

I sprinkled the rump roast with pepper and salt and rubbed it with flour. Then I fried the salt pork in our Dutch oven until it was crisp, and placed the meat in to brown.

Usually I can talk to Rob about most things. Both of us have found this school year the pits. There's so much propaganda in the early high school years about how seniors get the run of the school and don't have to do much work because they are practically graduated; none of it is true. Between SATs and applications and that great spreading void inside that comes of not knowing what will happen to you next year, senior year is hardest of all.

The phone rang again. I let it ring. But it kept on ringing, and I knew it was Rob. I picked up the receiver.

"Amy, they're *your* scores. *You* open the envelope."

"You might not want to know me when you hear how badly I did."

"Will you come on? What do I care about your SAT scores? I know how smart you are."

"That kind of smart is not worth anything."

"Amy Bloomer Hamilton, will you stop with that self-pity?"

"Don't you dare call me that stupid name." Anger took the

place of sorrow and I found my strong voice again. "You know how much I hate it. I'm in the middle of trying a recipe and I can't stop to talk."

"Amy, open the letter. Please."

"All right, all right. But don't start saying things to comfort me. Not one word. Promise you won't say anything."

"All right. I promise."

I left him waiting, and moved very slowly to get the letter and then to get Mother's letter opener, and then to slip it under the flap. I moved as if great weights were holding me back.

"Rob?"

"Still here. I've had a good nap."

"The Jackpot losing numbers in today's Connecticut Lottery are 500 in English; 400 in math." My knees were dissolving, so I sat down.

"Not too terrible, Amy—" he started.

"You promised," I cried, and hung up.

I went back to my cooking. The roast had browned beautifully. I added a little boiling water to cover the bottom of the pot along with a bay leaf, parsley, and the currants. Then I set it to simmer slowly. While I was doing this the phone rang insistently, but I didn't answer. After a long while, it stopped. I was sorry to treat Rob that way, but I just couldn't help myself. Some things just can't be discussed.

Perhaps this sounds like I am making far too much out of that envelope and its contents, but that's not so. For the last year and a half or so, test scores have been the major, and practically the only, subject in my home, my school, and my

24

life. A subject I never brought up. Even when Uncle George calls from New York these days, he hints about my scores, indirectly. "What's the bad news? Forget Ivy; it's all poison anyway. This country is full of excellent small colleges." He starts to list alternatives.

At that point, Mother usually grabs the phone and tells him Bennington is the school of choice. I have overheard him scolding her for her "obsession" and telling her she was being unrealistic and unfair to push me. But she never listens.

Seniors aren't people; they're test scores.

All of this is only part of a larger problem, which is that since my junior year I've had the oddest feelings about school. It's as if I'm a tightrope walker required to appear and do my act every school day. What's going on all around me seems so remote, so boring and unrelated to what's happening to my body and inside my mind, that I have to concentrate extremely hard on keeping my balance and just getting through the performance. Which is the school day.

I am a B—/C+ student just as Uncle George was. The difference between us is that he could have done better if he'd cared—Mother says he has an agile mind—but I am doing the *best* that I can. An examophobe is a handicapped person. My mother eats her heart out over my grades. She tutors me. She encourages me and challenges me. But one way or the other she talks about it all the time.

"You're very much like your father," she says. "He was a private, abstracted person. Not a world-beater. Men who major in English literature are rarely world-beaters." And her green eyes get that distant look, and she's removed from

25

me, reminiscing. "Your grandfather nearly had a heart attack when Thomas Hamilton, who was not even a regular church-goer, came calling." She sums it all up triumphantly. "He sent me to a teachers' college. I was bound to meet a teacher and marry him."

Mother loved Daddy; no question about that. She just got a little extra bonus because marrying him paid Grandfather back.

"Your father was a private, introspective person. He had no business on a motorbike. With his reflexes he belonged in an armored car," she jokes bitterly. "You would have loved him, Amy, as he dearly loved you."

I was mopping off the counter where I'd been working, my eyes all blurry, oblivious to everything but my own misery, when a voice from right behind me said, "What a mess you're making. Why don't you wipe your eyes?"

I jumped at the sound and landed on Rob's right foot. "My eyes are tearing because I was slicing onions."

"I understand." He stood one-legged like a stork and rubbed his injury. "Mine are tearing from the sudden ampu-tation of my toes."

"Sorry. How did you get in here?"

"Your keys were still in the front-door lock." He dangled them before me and then put them down on the table. "You look terrible. Go wash your face or something."

The bathroom mirror confirmed it. My eyes were blood-shot and swollen, and my pale skin was blotchy. I had thoroughly disheveled my hair by pushing my fingers through it a hundred times. I looked like a miserable twelve-

26

year-old. Using icy water, I doused my face and then I combed my hair. These were minor improvements; they had nothing to do with the misery in my mind.

"Come and sit down with me for a minute," Rob said, reaching for my hand.

"I have to finish cleaning up here."

"A minute or two. That's all."

He sat me on a kitchen chair, and brought one for himself and set it close to me.

"Now," he said, "tell me what the big tragedy is all about."

I said dully, "You know."

"Your scores aren't high. So you won't go to Bennington."

"Bennington doesn't particularly care about scores, and you know I wasn't going there anyway."

"I thought I knew that. But then what is it that's got you all upset?"

"My mother will be miserable about my scores. She'll want me to be tutored. Or to take a cram course. Then I'll have to take the exam again. And I don't want to! I don't want to go to college next year just to say I've been. I don't want to go just because everyone else is going."

"Then don't go."

"Hah! Easy to say."

Rob frowned. "I don't understand *why* you don't want to go, Amy." I moved to get up, but he held me there. "I mean, I've heard all the things you've said, but you don't really have anything else you're dying to do. What will you do next year when all of us—all the seniors—are gone? The town will be dead."

27

"I'll find something I want to do."

"That's too vague. It would be sensible to make some plans, to go away, to have some goal."

"I thought you were on my side."

"I am. I just mean you can't go on saying you don't want to go to college. You have to start saying you *do* want to do something else."

"I want to do something *I* want to do."

"Like what?"

"Like cooking—or sewing—or learning to weave rugs on a loom. Something that involves my hands *and* my brain."

"Now we're getting somewhere," Rob said.

"Where?" I laughed. "You think my mother will let me do those things?"

"Not if *you* suggest them. Go tell them to Mr. O and let him help."

"You know, Rob," it suddenly occurred to me, "he met me in the hall today and urged me to come and see him. Do you think he knew my scores before I did?"

"No. But he wouldn't have to. He knows about you and tests."

"What can he do for me?"

"It can't hurt to see him. And he just might come up with something."

"Okay, I'll go see him. But what about you, Rob? What will you do?"

It was his turn to look glum.

"You know, you could've gotten lower scores."

"That would have been another kind of cheating. I'd have

cheated myself. Anyway, Amy, I don't want lower scores, because *I want* to go on studying. I just don't want to study medicine. With my grades and a good portfolio, I could probably study art at Yale, except it would have to be over my father's dead body. So I'll have to do it elsewhere."

The cuckoo in our kitchen clock warned us it was five o'clock. I didn't want Rob around when Mom came home and got the news. "Rob, I have to finish cleaning up."

"And I'm due back home. Listen"—he chucked me under the chin—"remember it's not the end of the world."

"It's not?"

"Nope." He bent down and kissed the top of my head. "I promise you, Amy Bloomer Hamilton, for us there is life after the SATs."

"Not long for you if you call me by that name, Rob."

Speedily, he went.

6

At five-thirty, when my mother came home, the simmering stage was over, and the aroma from the Dutch oven was a delight. But I did not start the final step, preparing and adding the turnips, carrots, and potatoes. My Yankee Pot Roast would make a fantastic dinner, I knew, and I also knew it was doomed for this evening. In our house we feasted or we fought, but we never combined the two activities.

"Hi, honey." Mom kissed my cheek, and then kicked off her shoes. She feels that being short is a handicap for a teacher, so she always wears high heels to work. "A tall teacher has a psychological advantage," she argues. "About eight feet tall is the perfect height."

As if she needed a psychological advantage. My mother is unusually pretty and very smart. She practically dominates any room that she's in. I guess it's charisma (SAT word), or something, but she never has any serious discipline problems in her classes. And not because she wears high heels. Because she's steel underneath the petite disguise. That's my problem: she's steel underneath, and I, who look just like her, am oatmeal underneath.

"What a day," she said. "The School Board notified me that there isn't enough money in the budget to print the magazine. They suggest we mimeograph it. Mimeograph! Not even Xerox. And what are we supposed to do with all those lovely, delicate drawings Rob did? Mimeograph them? The Board has money for football and basketball and wrestling and a million coaches for afterschool activities, but money for the one important intellectual activity—the literary magazine—that money they don't have."

"Gee, I'm sorry, Mom. What will you do?"

"I don't know. I know what I won't do. I *won't* mimeograph. That's an insult to all of our work. I'm thinking of calling Uncle George and asking him to come and visit next weekend. We haven't seen him in ever so long. And he knows lots about printing and publishing. Maybe he can come up with some inexpensive ways, though the Board claims it has absolutely nothing at all to give us."

"Good idea." Uncle George would help her, and his presence might also help me in my predicament because one thing about Uncle George, he is cool. He is the living definition of the word. He is positively chill.

My mother's eye focused on the mantel. "Scores come?"

"Yes."

"How'd you do, honey? I sure need some good news today.

31

Come on, give me a pick-me-up." Her deep green eyes gleamed with anticipation.

"Not so well, Mom," I mumbled.

"Amy? What does 'not so well' mean?" A shrillness came into her voice. "Translate that into numbers, please."

"You're sure you want to hear?" I was scared. She had come home feeling down. I didn't want to make it worse.

"They couldn't be *that* bad. Come on, baby. How'd you do?"

"English: 500; math: 400."

She drew in breath as if she were in pain, and then she sat down. "There's probably been a computer error," she said slowly. "I simply don't believe those scores. Not the math score, anyway. You'd never get a 400 in math. Not after all the tutoring I paid for."

I felt exactly as helpless as I had felt that first time in first grade when my phobia was discovered. Helpless and full of panic. "Mom—the day I took the exam—remember? I told you how hard it was."

She wasn't listening to me. "Look. They *give* you 200 to start out with even if you don't get a single question right. How could you get only 400 out of 800?"

"I'm lousy in math."

"I won't hear that." She glared at me, her teacher glare, as if she could penetrate my skull and burn her determination into my brain. "You listen to me, young lady. You have an excellent mind. A first-class mind. And a high IQ. A lot of support from me here at home. Don't tell me you can't do

32

math. I don't believe it. It's a feminine weakness to think that math is impossible. Anyone can do math."

"I can't take tests," I said. "I hate them. I go in all prepared and then I'm paralyzed." There was no use in my talking. She knew all this but she did not understand it.

She got up and put her arms around me and hugged me and smoothed my hair back. "Don't worry about it. Tomorrow I'll call them in Princeton, and I'll bet I find out it's all a mistake. It's happened before. Their computers aren't infallible, you know." She paused. "And if you froze on this exam and didn't do well—if it turns out this nightmare is not a mistake—why, then you can take the SATs again. And we can register you for a cram course. I'll help you. That English score is not your true score either. I *know* it's not. You write beautifully. You can raise it to 550 easily."

Bennington's level is 550.

I began to cry.

"Don't cry, darling," she begged. "Please don't. It will all be all right. Mother will straighten it out."

How to make her understand? How?

"The house smells of some wonderful cooking," she said, "but I'm really not feeling hungry after all that hassle in school. Can we hold off on your delicacy until Friday night? Then maybe Uncle George will be here to enjoy it too."

I nodded. I would have choked if I'd had to eat just then.

Mom headed for the phone to call Uncle George, and I put the meat and gravy into a plastic container and stored it in the freezer. I was happy remembering that Jessie had said Yankee Pot Roast improves with standing.

Of course those *were* my scores.

Mom made the call the next day while I stood by, writhing. The Educational Testing Service must get a lot of these hysterical-parent calls. The telephone person was very systematic. Mom gave my name, address, social security number, and birthdate. There was a long wait while my records were being checked. Then came the bad news. Guess what? Mom heard they *were* my scores.

"Please check again," she said. "Hamilton is not an uncommon name, and these are extremely unlikely scores for my daughter, who is very gifted."

I nearly died listening to that.

In a moment the voice on the phone was talking again, assuring my mother that there were no errors. Amy Bloomer Hamilton had scored 500 and 400.

Mom had to let her go at last. Coming away from that phone call, she looked like she'd just heard I had terminal botulism. Her eyes glittered with tears. "You can take the tests again," she assured me. "Most seniors take them several times. It's no disgrace."

"I can't," I said.

"What do you mean, *can't*?"

"I mean I don't want to. I don't want to take the SATs again, ever. I'm not going to."

"Why not?"

"Because I'll *never* do that much better."

34

"You could take a cram course."

"No, I can't."

She looked really beat. "Why are you determined to be a failure?" she asked me. "I want to do everything I can for you so you can have a wonderful, rich, cultured life. And whatever I suggest, you turn down. Why?"

"Because you want me to do things *you* want. You want me to fulfill your dreams. I don't want the same things. I never wanted to go to Bennington—even if they'd have me, which is doubtful. I'm not a poet or an artist. I'm average. Who knows, I'm probably below average because average kids can take tests."

Her eyes blazed. "Don't say that."

"It's true. You might as well accept me. I'm not special."

"You are special to me." Suddenly she looked small and defeated, standing there in her stockinged feet. "If only I could understand what it is you want."

"I don't know."

"So, what will you do? After graduation, I mean?"

"Mom, you know many seniors aren't sure of what they want to do next. I'm just another one of them. *I don't know!*"

"I've offered therapy. I've offered counseling. I'll do anything I can to help you." She was stricken with guilt, as though my indecision was her fault. It was, but in quite a different way. The harder she pushed, the more I balked.

"Amy, baby, all I want is to help you. Any normal mother wants that."

"The best thing you can do for me is leave me alone. Have faith in me and let me work things out."

"It's hard," she said.

"I know."

"I just can't." Her voice faltered.

"You'll have to." I went to her and put my arms around her, and we wept together. "Why don't you go upstairs and work on the Great American Novel for a while," I suggested, "and forget all about me."

She went, grateful for the momentary escape.

7

Uncle George was glad to come. The pace of his life in the city was too fast for him, but he couldn't seem to slow things down. He drove up in his new Volvo station wagon, metallic blue with black trim. Neat! I love seeing him: tall, sophisticated in his London Fog trenchcoat, or a tweedy jacket, or a cashmere sweater and button-down shirt. He has the family black hair, but his eyes are changeable hazel. Sometimes he looks like Jeremy Irons, whom I adore, but Uncle George smiles more. He is my idea of how to use the term *model*: Uncle George, not Amelia Bloomer.

"How're my—uh—women?" he asked, gathering us in for a joint hug. He used to say *girls* till Mom cured him of that. Nobody calls her a girl and escapes. She says it's a condition she's long since outgrown, and it was the worst time of her life.

"I'm so glad you invited me," he said. "I haven't been here in ever so long." He settled down on the couch with a glass of sherry.

"Whose fault is that?" Mom asked.

"Actually it's Chiara's fault."

"Who?"

"I have this girlfr—woman friend, Chiara."

"Chiara?" Mom said. "What kind of name is that?"

"A made-up kind. Her name is really Lene. From Magdelene."

I giggled. It was all so complicated. When I got around to changing my name, I hoped no one would ask me what it was before. That would spoil it all. Suppose when I was Topaz or Monica, or any one of the other glamorous names, people asked and found out I was Amelia before. The change wouldn't have done much good.

"Lene is a good Italian name," he said, "but Chiara has more style. Anyway, she's a jogger and she talked me into it. I am so healthy and tired and musclebound—"

"Why don't you say, 'No thank you'?" Mom suggested.

"Nobody says 'no' to Chiara. She's a stockbroker with a seat on the Exchange. Gorgeous, but Ms. Assertiveness Training herself."

Mom smiled. "George, you always find such unlikely women."

"That's what keeps me free."

"Where'd you meet her?" I was curious.

"Actually, I met her in the cheese department of Luigi's, my favorite gourmet shop. I was in agony trying to decide between mozzarella and Gorgonzola."

"That's so romantic," I said, making them both laugh. "Which did you buy?"

38

"Both, at Chiara's recommendation. Then it turned out her brother owned the shop."

Mom and I hooted at that.

He nodded. "I accused her of being a shill. But the cheeses were excellent. Now all three of us are friends." He sipped his sherry. "But I've talked enough. Tell me your news."

"I bombed on the SATs," I said, before Mom could turn it into a five-act tragedy. Shakespeare was her specialty.

"How lethal were the bombs?"

"English: 500; math: 400."

He was cool. "Looks like you won't be a National Merit Finalist, kid." He stroked my hair. "Don't take it too hard. Those are respectable scores—nothing flashy, but nothing to be ashamed of."

"You know what those scores mean, George?" Mom's voice was high and thin, the way it gets when she's edgy.

"Yeah. They mean that your solemn, insane vow will now have to go up the spout. But it went long ago, Doris, long long ago. Amy is a terrific kid, beautiful, bright, sensitive. But she is not right for the *Ahrts*."

"You don't know," Mom said, "and we aren't giving up so fast. She can take the exams again."

"For heaven's sake, Doris," Uncle George said impatiently, leaning forward over his knees, "put your energy where it should go. Finish your novel and let me read it. Or send it to a publisher. Take a trip. Dye your hair pink. *Do something real!* Tom's been dead for fifteen years."

"We'll talk more about this another time, George."

"I'll look forward to it. What else is happening?"

"The School Board just cut out the budget for the *Pen & Ink*."

"You mean cut the budget."

"No. They cut it out entirely. They feel if the students want a magazine they should find ways to pay for it."

"Philistines! Do the football and baseball and basketball teams have to find ways to pay for their uniforms and equipment?"

"Who are the Philistines?" I asked.

"People without taste," Uncle George said. "Clods. What will you do, Doris?"

"I don't know yet. We'll publish somehow."

"Well," Uncle George said, "I'm glad you asked me up this weekend so I can relax. Get away from all the urban tensions. It's worse here than it is in New York."

"Amy has made us a special dinner," Mom said, " a new version of Yankee Pot Roast."

"A new old version," I said. "It dates back to colonial days."

Uncle George perked up. He's an eater, six feet two inches of carnivore. "What could anyone do with that plain and sensible New England dish?"

"Wait and see."

"Where'd you come upon such a find, Amy?"

"Jessie," I said. "Jessie Campbell. She teaches Home Ec part-time in our high school. She took over that old grocery near the bank and renamed it Colonial Cookery. She sells some groceries and terrific baked goods. She has a stereo going soft in the background, Beethoven to Beatles, and she's writing this cookbook. She is the most incredible cook."

"She is," Mom agreed. "Jessie is something special."

"You'd like her, Uncle George. She was married but it didn't work out. She has a daughter my age, Jan. You'd like Jessie a lot. She's pretty and smart and she could cook up even a pot of grass and make it taste good."

"Grass?" Uncle George repeated doubtfully.

"Grass grass—not pot. Real grass."

"Well, I think I have to meet her, don't I?"

"Yes," I said. "You'll find her restful. She doesn't jog. Mostly she hangs around the store cooking and baking, or she interviews local women on their recipes."

"You're very persuasive," he said. "She ought to hire you to sell. I hope the store has evening hours."

"Friday nights she stays open till ten."

"After dinner then," Uncle George proposed, "we'll take a walk so I can meet your friend."

Dinner was a ball. The Yankee Pot Roast looked terrific on our old blue china platter surrounded by chunks of turnips, carrots, and potatoes, and the currants definitely made a difference. We had a spectacular spinach salad and baked apples crammed with raisins and cinnamon and brown sugar. Uncle George had brought a chocolate cake from Eclair that had frosting an inch thick. The best part of the whole dinner was that not once—*not once*—did anyone mention SATs, graduation, or college. The big problem was how to finance *Pen & Ink*, and Uncle George promised to

41

look into inexpensive ways of printing it for us as soon as he got back home.

Mom was too bushed to walk with us, so after the dishes were done Uncle George and I went out together. It was a clear Connecticut night and the sky was ablaze with stars.

"It's lovely up here," Uncle George said. "Whenever I come to visit, I wonder why I live in the city."

"Discos," I said. "Restaurants, theaters, Bloomingdale's, bookshops, and all the excitement. That's why you live there."

"Yes," he agreed. "The ideal thing would be to have my apartment in the city and a small place up here too. It's easy enough to come back and forth."

"A *pied-à-terre*," I said, dragging the words up from this week's French vocabulary list.

Uncle George looked impressed. "The French is coming along, eh? *Depuis quand étudiez-vous le français?*"

"*J'étudie le français depuis trois ans et je le parle bien,*" I said.

Uncle George hugged me. "Terrific!"

"I speak okay, but I can't pass a written grammar test. I'm the only one in the class who gets tested orally."

"Most Frenchmen couldn't pass a written grammar test either," he said.

"Uncle George, you don't have to act as if I'm normal."

He looked at me curiously. "But you are normal, Amy."

"No, I'm not. Normal people can take normal tests. I can't."

42

"Is that your way of judging normality: who can take tests?"

"It's not my way. It's everybody else's."

"No," Uncle George protested, "not *every*body else's." He spoke strongly, as though he really meant what he said. "I don't accept that definition, and neither should you. People are born with different strengths and weaknesses. Who decides what's normal? Who makes the rules? Whoever does is not always fair—or smart. *You* have to decide what *your* personal standards are. That's the only way to operate."

This conversation was about the issue most on both our minds, but it was skirting it instead of talking about it directly. What we were really discussing was: my scores, my immediate future, and my destiny!

"Amy, I want to help. I just don't know how."

"No one can help, Uncle George. Mom is determined to push me into college. And I have made up my mind not to go."

"Then someone does have to help. Your mother loves you very much, you know."

"Of course I know it. And I love her too. But that's not the issue."

He nodded.

"I'm going to do what *I* want to do."

"Which is?"

"That's the trouble. I'm not sure yet."

"That's fair enough," he said, "at seventeen. It took me years to find out what I like to do and can do well. But I had a father to pay my way."

"That's part of it. I don't want Mom to pay my way any-where. Why should she pay for cram courses and college applications? And then pay college tuition? And, of course, she had to pick Bennington, probably the most expensive college in the country."

"She'd pay it gladly, Amy."

"Don't I know it? But they wouldn't have me, and I wouldn't want them."

We walked along in silence. The beauty of the clear brisk night was soothing.

"You need professional advice," Uncle George said. "Is Jim O'Brien still doing college advising for the school?"

"Who else?"

"He's the man for you, Amy. I never met a more direct person in my life. He's a rare bird in education, a first-rate college counselor."

"Okay. I'll go see him."

"If I were you, I'd go on my own, quickly, before your mother gets to him, because she'll present the case as she sees it, and it will be a different case."

"He knows a lot of it already."

"Yes," Uncle George said, and then he added sadly, "your mother should have married him ten years ago."

We were approaching Colonial Cookery. "Subject closed," I said, and he nodded.

8

"Breathe in, Uncle George," I ordered. "Jessie's baking, so there are bound to be discards." As I opened the heavy glass door I recognized . . . double chocolate brownies for the Saturday morning trade. Perfect timing.

Uncle George looked around the small store appreciatively: three walls were lined with shelves of goods and the fourth was a plate-glass window. Four small, round, white ice cream tables with chairs stood in an open corner for customers who wanted coffee or hot chocolate along with Jessie's pastries. A big, old-fashioned glass case, nearly empty now, would be filled tomorrow with fresh baked goods and incredibly sinful candies. Jessie had installed two Tiffany-style hanging lights but otherwise kept the store's old features: the dark wooden floor and the ancient cash register, which is gigantic. It's really a fun store to be in.

Jan was behind the counter in what Mom calls our "androgyny uniform": tight Levis, no belt, loose oxford shirt with the sleeves rolled up. Jan has short curly hair, a snub nose, and blue eyes; she and her mother are tall, lean, graceful women with the most beautiful complexions I've ever seen, creamy white and perfect.

"Hi, Jan. Meet my Uncle George."

"Amy never told me you were so—" Jan stared at him.

"Yes?" he encouraged.

"—yummy," she said, and began to giggle.

"She keeps me hidden because she's afraid I'll be devoured." Uncle George did his best to look very earnest.

"I don't think you're yummy," I said skeptically. "I think you're just passing."

"Speaking of just passing, Amy," Jan said. "I got my scores."

"Did I ever choose a terrible weekend to come visiting," Uncle George groaned.

"I *thought* I didn't do too well," Jan said. "Now I know it."

"I got my scores too. Terrible."

"English: 680; math: 550," Jan said.

"Better than me. Mine are English: 500; math: 400."

"If only it wasn't so important," Jan said, despairing. Then, fiercely, she added, "It shouldn't be so important!"

"It's not so important," I said.

"Yes, it is. I need financial aid if I'm going to college, and those scores will get me zilch. I have to boost them up. I'm going to have to take my savings from last summer's camp job and blow them on that cram course they give in New Haven."

"Oh, no!" I said. Those savings were earmarked for senior luxuries her mother couldn't afford to provide: yearbook, ring, photographs, graduation dress, all the pleasures of the coming spring. "That money is for other stuff."

"Yeah," she said, "I know. You going to join me in the cram course? We could suffer together."

"No thanks, Jan. I'm not taking those exams again, ever."

Jessie poked her head in from the kitchen. "I *thought* I heard voices." She really looked beautiful, all rosy from the heat of the oven. She was in the androgyny uniform too.

"Jessie, this is my Uncle George," I said. "Uncle George, meet Jessie Campbell."

They looked at each other, and, I know no one will ever believe this because it only happens in movies and Silhouette novels, but I swear, there was an electric shock, a jolt. I could sense it.

"I'm happy to meet you," Jessie said. "You're the New York uncle Amy is so fond of, the one who loves the city so."

"Yes," he said, "but when I get up here it's so beautiful and quiet I begin to have second thoughts."

"City people feel that way for about a weekend," Jessie said. "Then the quiet gets to them and it's too much. I've watched it all my life. It's metabolism, I think." She turned to Jan. "You can put the lights out now, honey, and lock up. No one in Eastfield is going to come out grocery shopping anymore tonight. Then"—she was looking at Uncle George—"why don't you all join me in the kitchen?"

Uncle George sniffed. "Free samples?"

"Of course. Burned and damaged brownies."

"They're the best," I said, "the rejects."

We had a lovely time eating brownie discards as we sat

around the big oak kitchen table helping Jessie with little chores like setting the cooled cakes on display trays and then covering them carefully with plastic wrap. Uncle George was sort of quiet, though he ate enthusiastically. He just watched Jessie as she worked competently and quickly, listening to her and asking an occasional question. She told him about herself. I learned a lot I didn't know. Jan and I are good friends, but we're private people about family.

Jessie was thirty-seven. She had married a college class-mate, who wanted to be a sociologist, and worked at all sorts of crummy jobs and raised Jan while he studied until he had his doctorate.

"Then Mike couldn't get a teaching job," Jessie said, deftly running her big serrated knife through the pan of cake in straight lines. "He looked everywhere, and he's a superb sociologist, but there were no jobs. He turned out to be one of those people who can't shift. All his life he'd wanted to be a college teacher, and when he couldn't do better than pick-ing up a course here and there, part-time, that's what he settled for. He wouldn't try anything else. He drinks too much and he works just enough not to starve."

"Does he do any writing?" my uncle asked. "Does he do research?"

She shook her head. "He does nothing but teach his part-time courses and mourn. He hopes something will open up. I couldn't take it after a while, so I got out. He's a good man. He misses Jan; he loves her dearly."

"How could he help it?" Jan asked, arranging brownies.

"Let me tell you—" I began, and she took a harmless poke

48

at me. She was always going up on the bus to Boston to visit her father; she was crazy about him. I think in a way it may be really worst of all to have parents who've split up but both of whom are nice. Because then you must spend a lot of time wondering why they couldn't make it together. Without a villain it's much harder to explain catastrophe.

When the brownies were done and the pans washed and the kitchen in good order, we said good night. But not before Uncle George got Jessie to agree to go for a walk after she closed the door on Saturday night.

"Eightish," she suggested.

"Perfect."

He and I walked home through the sleeping town silently. I was so glad he liked Jessie. Now if Mr. O could only convince Mom, we'd have double wedding bells, and I'd have taken care of all the adults in my life and I could be on my way.

Silent walks on starry country nights lead to this kind of fairy-tale dreaming.

9

Monday morning was foggy and gray; visibility was poor so that cars had to drive with their lights on. The kids coming in to school were damp and subdued like the weather. A clammy day. Perfect for me to go and see my college guidance counselor.

During my study hall period I set out to see Mr. O and ran into Rob on my way. He looked really down.

"Hi, Rob. What's happening?"

"You don't want to ask that," he warned me.

"Yes. I do." He was silent. "I'm asking," I said.

"Okay. I suggested to my folks that if Yale takes me I'd like to major in art. I didn't have to mention it because declaring a major comes later on—like in the second year—but I wasn't going to pretend medicine and then pull a switch. Well, we had a big confrontation scene. Dad exercising control for about ten seconds, then shouting. Me shouting. Mother clucking in the background, scared to death. Father wants to pass along the holy caduceus to son and son refuses.

Ungrateful son. Breaker of an illustrious line of Yale medical men."

"Sounds awful. What was the final outcome?"

Rob took off his glasses and rubbed his eyes wearily. He really looked shot, as though he hadn't slept in days. "If I go to college and I plan to major in anything but science, he doesn't see that he should pay for it."

"Rob!"

"He's got the courage of his convictions. Medicine is his life. 'Consider, Robert, consider how I feel having two sons neither of whom show the slightest curiosity or interest in what I love most.'

"'But Dad, don't take it personally,' I tried to tell him. 'It's just that science is not my thing.'

"'How do you know? Have you tried to make it *your thing*? Have you taken chemistry and physics and biology? Have you really given science a chance?'

"'No, because there are other subjects I would rather study, subjects I love as much as you love science.'

"'And you tell me not to take it personally. There is no other way to take it.'

"I've never seen him look so down," Rob said desolately. "Never. Even when Pete left, he had some hope. He had me to bank on."

"What does he expect you to do now?"

"He says I should stay an adolescent like my brother and go play baseball for a living."

The whole thing was so unfair. Dr. Burton had plenty of money to pay Rob's college tuition.

"What will you do, Rob?"

"I'll probably have to forget about Yale. SUNY Purchase or U. Conn, will do fine. Because my father is well-off, it won't be easy for me to get loans, but I've got some money saved and I can work. That kind of tuition is manageable."

"Will he really *not pay* your tuition? I mean—it sounds like something from my grandfather's time or before. Father cuts off disobedient son."

"Who knows? He's terribly hurt. If I don't take his well-meant paternal advice, I might well be on my own."

"Is that what he did with Pete?"

"Yes. But Pete is okay, making money. No problem there. And he'd had it with school. He wasn't a bad student but the pressure was always on. One thing they should teach in New Haven: freedom of choice for alumni kids."

"What a mess," I said. "I'm sorry, Rob." I thought about my own situation. "Mom is miserable about me and my not wanting to go to college, but she's never threatened to cut off support. I think she'd help me if she knew there was something I wanted to do."

"You have to understand. Medicine is the only thing Dad ever wanted to do. *Ever.* He can't see how Pete and I couldn't want it as well. He's convinced that we've rejected *him.*"

I checked my watch. "I've got to see Mr. O in three minutes."

Rob smiled. "I'm just coming from there now."

"Okay," I said, "try me."

"Mr. O was in rare form. I'll give you a clue. These first two are oldies: 'Beulah, peel me a grape.' "

"Easy," I said, "because it's so famous. Mae West in *I'm No Angel*."

He nodded. "I got that one, and the next too. 'What? From Africa to here, $1.85? That's an outrage. I told you not to take me through Australia!' "

"Groucho as Captain Spalding in *Animal Crackers*."

"Yes," Rob said. "This last quote is from a more recent picture. And it relates to me: 'Human see, human do.' "

"*Planet of the Apes*," I said. "Aside from evolution, how does it relate to you?"

"Ah. Mr. O wants me to listen to those apes and learn from them. He says I have to go my own way and work out my own destiny no matter how difficult that might be, and while I'm doing it I have to try to hurt my father as little as possible. So, human see and then human go quietly the other way."

"You father won't thank him for that advice."

"I told him that. Mr. O says he's sorry but that's irrelevant. A counselor is supposed to give students the best help he can, and Mr. O is satisfied that this is the best he can do for me. He told me not to give it another thought. He has tenure."

"I'd better go see him," I said.

"The Force be with you."

"You too, friend," I said fervently. "You too."

10

Mr. O was waiting for me in his fifth floor office. The little room was, as always, packed with catalogues and propaganda from colleges, most of it real but some of it Hollywood. My favorite poster was of Groucho Marx as President Wagstaff of Huxley College from the movie *Horsefeathers*. There was also a neat one of President Reagan in football uniform from *Knute Rockne*. The real college posters were of perfect young men and women frolicking on perfect green campuses. Their SAT scores were, no doubt, astounding.

"Hello, Hamilton, Amy B." Mr. O was sitting at his desk. I could see a quote coming. "Ready? 'There's no sense in being killed by a man-eating plant.'"

"*Day of the Triffids*," I said, without needing time to think.

He rose and came around the desk to seat me. He doesn't walk; he lumbers. Many years ago he used to come around to our house all the time, and take Mom and me to the movies, but then he ended up wanting to marry Mom. She wouldn't. She was too busy dedicating herself to me. So he stopped coming around and ended up marrying nobody.

Uncle George was right. Mom should have married him. He's the best thing about Eastfield High. It's to him that students go when everything and everyone else fails. Unofficially, he handles pregnancies, divorcing parents, cop problems, drugs, and other matters. Mostly he tries to handle them off the record. He respects students' privacy. Maybe it's because he trained to be a priest for years before he decided he didn't have a calling.

"How's it going, Amy B?" he asked me.

"It's not going so well, Mr. O."

"I don't know why I ask that question," he said, more to himself than to me. "Eleven out of ten seniors answer in the negative." He smiled at me. "Sit. Let's try another one. 'A gun's a tool, Marion. No better and no worse than the man who uses it.' "

"*Shane*," I said. "You give me ones that are too easy."

"Oh, yes?" He put his hands palm to palm upright and rested his chin on them, and thought. " 'Why do we do this?'/ 'You got to do something, don't you?' "

"Mr. O, they're too simple."

"I'm waiting."

"*Rebel Without a Cause*. James Dean and the other kid, before the car bit."

He looked at me sternly. "You've been going to too many movies, young woman." We both laughed.

"All right," he said. "What brings you here before I sent

for you? You seniors think a college adviser has nothing to do but see seniors." He was fooling around, trying to be upbeat, but it didn't work.

"I got my SAT scores, Mr. O."

"And they are?"

"English: 500; math: 400."

He sat his chin on the tips of his fingers again, pursed his lips, and looked at me thoughtfully for a long time. "Well," he said at last, "actually you didn't do badly at all. Actually, you did well. You're a smart girl and a terrible test-taker. These are not *terrible* scores at all."

"Try to tell that to my mother."

He sighed, then he spoke carefully, deliberately. "Your mother will hate me for this, Amy, but I do not see a snob college in your future. I see some perfectly pleasant and respectable little liberal arts colleges. But they do not include the giants."

"Can we count out Bennington as a giant?" I asked hopefully. "If they won't have me, I can't go, and that's that."

He scratched his head over one ear. "Hard to say. They take creative people and they don't worry about formal credentials. It's probably the one select school in the country where SAT scores are really not that important."

"My luck."

"Well, Amy, they count the personal interview and the essays on their application as most important. You speak well and are personable. Of course, I've never interviewed you for college. If you didn't freeze up you could do very well. And, English test scores to the contrary, you are quite a good

56

writer. So, it's possible you could get in. They're looking for creative people, not conventional good students."

"Creative people means what?"

"In music, dance, writing, theater. In the graphic arts. People who sincerely want to expand. To stretch."

"How about cooking?" I asked him. "How about knitting, rug-making, embroidery? How about those arts, Mr. O?"

"I don't believe those are Bennington arts, Amy. We can study the catalogue and I can make inquiries if you like. But those are more traditional domestic arts, and Bennington is not really the place for them."

"Don't bother inquiring, Mr. O. I don't really want to go to college."

"Funny," he said, "I had the impression that going there was your—kismet."

"I wonder where you got that impression."

He smiled. "I thought you went along with it. Actually, I tried to tell your mother years ago that she was being unrealistic. I tried, and your uncle tried. She didn't want to hear us. We had some fierce arguments over it." He paused. "You know I'm still very fond of your mother."

"I know. And she likes you too. She's just got these screwball notions about me."

He nodded, and then began blurrily to whistle.

" 'As Time Goes By,' " I said. "*Casablanca*."

"Who plays it?"

"That's easy. Sam."

"Uh-huh. Name of the actor?"

It happens I'm a Humphrey Bogart freak and I know

practically everything about his movies. Not so many people would have come up with this one. "Dooley Wilson."

With his thumb and forefinger, Mr. O made a perfect circle of congratulations and tossed it my way. "They shouldn't let teachers' children attend the school where their parents teach. It's too sticky. But I'll tell you what I'm going to do for you. I'm going to advise you as if you were Miss Average American Student, personally unknown to me. As if I didn't even know your mother. I would advise a two-year community college or a small liberal arts college, a fairly relaxed noncompetitive school. I think you'd have a very good time and you'd get a good education. That is—if that's what you want."

"*I don't want to go to college, Mr. O,*" I repeated. I understood that after all the years of my mother's brainwashing, he hadn't quite gotten my message yet. "At least not in the immediate future. Not for a few years."

He began to build church steeples with his fingers as he absorbed that. I could see it didn't penetrate easily. Teachers' kids go to college. Kismet is not easily thwarted.

"All right, you tell me. What would you most like to do after graduation?"

"I'm not sure. I think I've had enough schooling for a while. I'm bored, Mr. O. Most of the stuff we cover in class doesn't mean much to me."

"Senioritis," he said.

"It was sophomoritis and junioritis too."

"Well, we can get some professional advice. See what your aptitudes are."

58

"I know what they are. All the wrong ones, according to Mom. She calls them slavey aptitudes: cooking, baking, needlework of all kinds. Those are the things that interest me."

He whistled another few lines of "As Time Goes By" with his odd hissing whistle, and accompanied himself by tapping his foot. Then he leaned over the desk and looked at me intently. "Have you told her?"

"I've tried a million times. She doesn't want to hear it."

"You aren't by any chance doing this just to punish your mother, are you, Amy? You aren't opting for all the things she hates just to show your independence?"

"That idea has occurred to me, and I've wondered about it a lot. I can honestly say I don't think so. It's possible that because she's always worked and I missed her at home that I became the kind of person I am. I've loved working in the kitchen since I was small. I'm good at cooking. I know I am, and Jessie Campbell says I am too. She says I'm talented."

"You are," he agreed. "I'm thinking of those meringues you baked for Open School Night. Formidable." He patted his ample middle. "You are dangerously good."

"Mr. O, I'm desperate," I said. "Mom called Princeton because she couldn't believe that those low scores were mine. She scolded the ETS person for insisting they *were* mine. It's like she doesn't know me at all, like I'm a stranger. I *never* do well on tests. *Never.* Why can't she admit that to herself?"

"Amy, I wish I could answer those questions. We have parents whose kids are strung out on drugs and they don't see it; they *can't* see it. Nor can some parents of kids who are alcoholics. There is something in being a parent that makes it very terrible to admit that your child is different, or has some slight flaws. Your mother is not the worst, believe me." He sighed. "I'll talk to her. Don't expect miracles, but I'll do what I can."

I nodded gratefully.

"The next few weeks are going to be particularly hard," he said. "In my experience, senior winter into early spring is the worst time in high school. It's limbo. You don't know where you are. Don't let it get to you."

"I'll do my best."

"Good. Because after that comes senior project time. Six weeks away from school to try your hand at something you like. We'll be posting opportunities soon. Come by and look them over."

"I will. Thanks for everything." I got up.

He dismissed my gratitude with a wave of his hand. " 'I stick my neck out for no one,' " he said thickly.

"Rick. *Casablanca.*"

"Those SAT people don't know nothin', kid." He was still Bogart. "You're smart. Take it from me. Smart!"

I left there smiling, but I was mindful of all that he'd said.

11

Mr. O was a prophet; those next weeks were just as he'd predicted. The worst!

First, for Rob.

His father did not give up easily. Rob had a terrible time with him over the selection of a senior project. Dr. Burton jumped the gun and, without consulting Rob or Mr. O, made arrangements for Rob to do his project as a volunteer in the Emergency Room of the County Consolidated Hospital. He came home all enthused with Rob's possibilities. "It will be interesting for you, son. Try it. Give it a month. Perhaps you'll learn to love it. Amazing cases come into the Emergency Room, and you'll be helping them. All kinds of people in distress. Everyone down there is keen on having my son there, learning."

"I wouldn't love it. I'd hate it," Rob protested. "It's not what I have in mind for *my* senior project. I want to do some art-related thing."

Dr. Burton made a face as if some bad smell had just filled the room. "What does that mean?"

"I want to work in a museum. Or help teach art in an elementary school. Or work with mental patients, helping them with their drawing and painting."

"You prefer that to working in the Emergency Room? I can't believe it. I don't understand how I can have two sons and no heirs. What I wanted most to share with you and Peter, neither of you has any use for."

"Sorry, Dad."

"So now I have to go back down to the hospital and tell them. I have to expose my shame. 'Sorry, folks. Robert won't be coming here after all to help the sick. He'd rather draw pictures with children and psychotics. Forget all about him.'"

"You shouldn't have volunteered me in the first place. I told you how I feel about medicine. I didn't want you to get me a project placement. We're supposed to get our own."

"I was merely trying to help you."

"To help me to do what *you* want me to do."

Dr. Burton was so angry he couldn't speak.

"Dad, I can't help it if my taste and talents—if I have any—lead me another way."

"I only ask you to give medicine a chance—for my sake."

"I just can't."

"You mean you don't want to."

"I guess that is what I mean."

"How do you know you don't want to? How do you know you don't like medicine? You've never really tried it. Working in the Emergency Room would give you a closer view than you've ever had."

"I don't need a closer view. Of medicine, or computers, or engineering, or ballet. I just *know* they are not for me. If I study, I do well in courses. That has nothing to do with whether I like them. I am *not* interested in medicine. I know it's a noble profession and I respect it. But it's not for me."

"You understand that I mean what I say about tuition? I will not waste one penny on art school. I am perfectly willing to bear the burden of a scientific education for you, but I will not throw money away on courses which can lead nowhere."

"I understand."

"And I shall forbid your mother to give you any money surreptitiously."

"I wouldn't take your money that way."

"I believe you. Nonetheless, nothing will come from her."
Rob nodded.

"If you should change your mind—" his father started, but Rob interrupted him, passionately.

"I won't change my mind. I won't ever change it. I'm your son, and the same stubbornness that inhabits you is in me. I'll go after what I want in my life."

"Then this is the last conversation on this subject that we shall have," his father said.

"Suits me." Rob felt like putting his hand forth, or touching his father's arm, but knowing he would be rebuffed he didn't try. He went to his room and found to his amazement

63

that his eyes were wet; he was crying for the first time since he was a small child.

"Dad couldn't bend and I wouldn't," he told me sadly, afterward. "What doesn't bend under pressure, breaks; I felt it happening. The split will be there between us now, forever."

12

Then it was my turn.

My mother stood in the doorway of my room, her arms folded across her chest. I knew she was there on serious business because she was wearing her high-heeled pumps. Two inches of extra height. Two inches of psychological advantage.

"Jim O'Brien talked to me after school today. I know you put him up to it."

"Not exactly. It was his idea. I had a conference with him earlier in the week, and he said at the end of it that he would speak to you."

"It would have been courteous if you had told me you were going to meet with him. Then we could have prepared for it."

That made me mad. "He's my college counselor, I didn't need to be *prepared* for him. I told him my scores. He asked what I wanted to do, what schools I was thinking of going to, and I told him."

"Good," she said grimly. "Now tell me."

"I've been trying to tell you for months. For years. My whole life practically, but you won't listen. And when you do actually listen, it's as if you can't hear me."

"That's what I'm doing now. Listening."

"Maybe now is too late."

"Don't get dramatic, Amy. I'm waiting."

How do you tell your mother the one thing she doesn't want to hear? Not easily. How do you soften it? No way I could think of.

"I don't want to go to school anymore. At least, not right away."

She stared at me. If I'd said, Mom, I'm pregnant out of wedlock, and the doctor says they're quintuplets, she couldn't have been more astounded. She stared at me, her pale face looking weary, discouraged.

"So, you're finished with school forever. You're smart enough, educated enough. You know everything."

"That's unfair. All I said was I don't want to go to college right away. I don't want to apply now. There are other things in this world."

"Like what?" she demanded. "What will you do? Work as a salesgirl, babysitter, clerk? Perfectly decent respectable jobs, but badly paid. Minimum wage jobs—is that what you want? You have no skills. Who will hire you?"

She paused.

I had no answers.

"You like to spend money," she said. "You like Frye boots and Laura Ashley dresses and beautiful sweaters. You like to

66

buy records and books. I don't blame you, but you won't be able to afford any of that."

She was running along like a steamroller. I had to stop her. "Mom, wait a minute," I protested. "I didn't say I don't *ever* want to learn anything again. I just don't want to run on to college because everyone else is doing it. I don't want to spend the next four years pretending I'm learning and I'm fascinated by all of it when I'm really bored."

"You're all of seventeen years old. What do you know yet about what's good for you?"

"You thought *you* knew when you were seventeen, and your father wouldn't let you choose. You've always resented that."

She sagged a bit. Her arms dropped to her sides. "That was totally different. He was unreasonable, a religious fanatic. It's cruel of you to throw that in my face."

"I don't mean to be cruel. It's necessary for me to mention it."

She seemed uncertain, moving slightly as if she was about to leave and then staying there.

"You can be sure," she said, her voice low and strained, "that I will never force you to do something you don't want to do. I would like to convince you; that's different from forcing you. Consider carefully. Even with your low scores you could get into a halfway decent school. Or you could take the cram course and pull those scores way up. I *know* you could. I *know* how smart you are when you want to be, Amy. You only have to put your head to your studies." She flashed me a wan smile of encouragement.

67

But she was wrong. She was voluntarily blind. I had honestly done the best that I could do on those exams. I'm not dumb. But I am no test-taker. In any competitive academic situation, I fail.

"Think how you'll feel next fall when all your classmates go away to school," she continued. "What will you do?"

I thought about it constantly, and I was scared. It's very hard to get off the track when you've been running along with everyone else all your life. Eastfield, Connecticut, is small and quiet, and once my friends took off I would be lonely. Some classmates would still be around, but not my friends. I was the only one I knew who wasn't looking forward to the day college or secretarial school or computer school began. Everyone was going somewhere!

I answered her honestly. "I don't know, Mom. I just don't know what I'll do. But I know what I *won't* do. I *won't* let you put money into an expensive cram course, and I won't make out an application and go and be interviewed at a place I'm not interested in."

She was silent. She cracked her knuckles, which she does whenever she is under severe tension. It drives me mad.

"Mom, don't do that."

"Sorry." She stopped. "It's dangerous, Amy. You may be left high and dry. Won't you at least apply? You can always defer admission, or not go at all. But just in case, apply."

Rob's father had tried that tactic on him too. Just apply and then when the time comes we'll see. You might change your mind. Et cetera, et cetera.

I shook my head. To apply would mean inevitably to go.

"Sorry, Mom, I would do it for you if it didn't mean my whole life. But that's what it means: my whole life!"

"And what about my life, which I've devoted to you? What about all those years of trying, of lessons and coaching?"

"I didn't ask you to do it. You wanted to."

"Whether or not you asked me doesn't matter. I did it because I'm your mother. I thought that you needed help and I gave it, gladly."

"And that made me the person that I am. I thank you for it."

"That's not enough," Mom said slowly. "A perfunctory 'I thank you for it' is not enough."

"It's not perfunctory. I never meant *anything* more. I'm very grateful to you. But I'm telling you now the way my life has to go."

She stood looking at me. She was dreadfully hurt, but I got the strangest feeling for the first time in my whole life that she was impressed. She understood that I had to cut free and move off in my own direction.

But where?

13

The bleakness continued.

Connecticut winters are long and harsh; they last, sometimes, right till summer. Early spring is a rare gift in Eastfield and we did without it my senior year. The days were long and cold and rainy, and the chill penetrated thick layers of clothing so I was numb all the time. My soul was cold. My relationship with Mom was at an impasse. We didn't talk about college anymore; in fact, we barely talked, and then it was *at* each other, politely. She was down in the dumps. Literally. She didn't go upstairs to write in the evenings anymore. She was just too depressed. And she wore far too much blush and eye shadow and bright 1940s lipstick. When she's happy, my mother doesn't need makeup. She's beautiful.

If she was down in the dumps, I was several levels below her. Never had I felt so hopelessly lost and trapped. It is one thing to declare independence bravely; it is quite another to know what the next step is. I was paralyzed. I could not take the next step. Everyone else ran about getting extra teacher recommendations, peer recommendations, adviser's recommendations. People put together portfolios, made tapes, and collected their best writings and hurried them off to college admissions offices. Jan was working away at the SAT cram course, and she'd sit at lunch poring over the idiot drills and occasionally consulting us.

"Guys—antonyms: *tyro*. (A) upstart, (B) veteran, (C) neophyte, (D) camper, (E) giant."

"That's B," Rob said, "veteran."

"One more?" she asked. "*Pariah*. (A) leper, (B) untamed animal, (C) celebrity, (D) outcast, (E) uncultured person."

"Mmm." Rob puzzled over them. "I'd guess C, celebrity. But I'm not positive."

"I'll check it out," Jan said. She was desperately determined to do well; scholarship grants depended on it. She had withdrawn from the Cheering Squad even though it was basketball season and she loved basketball, and twice she had to be excused from *Pen & Ink* editorial meetings so she could study. Senior year had become one monster preparing-for-the-test for her.

Rob was calm. He was counting on SUNY Purchase, and there was always our own state university as a fallback. He didn't care one bit about missing the Ivies and breaking the Burton tradition. His father was holding firm; he was courteous but cold to Rob at home. He simply would have nothing to do with an undergraduate art major; he wouldn't pay for it and he didn't want to hear about it.

71

I stayed by myself whenever I could, those days. I avoided people who wanted to talk about my future. When the mailman came, I hid; his friendly gossip would have destroyed me. I found myself crying a lot.

One afternoon Rob came by and insisted that I come out walking with him. I bundled up and went out into the grayness and mist of the Connecticut winter. The bare trees and stark landscape fit my mood. I was depressed, dumb. Mostly I listened to Rob as he talked about his plans. "I can work part-time and Pete is going to lend me some money. He's doing all right now. So I get to choose exactly the kind of education I want. Any subsidy from Dad would cost me more than it was worth."

"I wish I were as brave as you are."

"It's not bravery when you have no choice," he said. "I have no choice. What about you, Amy? I hardly see you these days. You disappear after school. Have you thought about something you want to do?"

"I've thought about many things. Sometimes I even think I'd be better off dead. It would solve so many problems." I hadn't meant to say that; it just came out involuntarily.

He stopped walking and put out his hand to stop me. He lifted my face so that I was looking directly at him. I began to cry.

"What kind of dumb thing is that to say?"

"I know it's crazy and I do my best to drive crazy ideas away, but they come back. Late at night when I can't sleep, or very early in the morning, or any time at all. They just come back into my head. It would be so peaceful. It would end all this misery. I just can't meet my mother's expectations. Ever, ever, ever." I was sobbing so heavily my body was shaking and I couldn't say more.

"I couldn't meet my father's expectations either, so I just stopped trying. It's not our fault. It's their fault, their crazy ambitions for us."

I did my best to control myself. I wiped my eyes and blew my nose and stopped sobbing. "I know you're going through a hard time, Rob, but it's not the same. You're smart and talented. You've had seventeen years of success. I've had seventeen years of failure."

He started to protest but I put my gloved hand up and covered his mouth.

"Mmm"—he made a funny face—"pure wool. Delicious."

"Don't talk. Let me finish. From the time I was a very small kid I always had the feeling that I was something of a disappointment to my mother. She never said so, and she did her best to hide it, but I knew." I swallowed hard, and the icy air unlocked months of words that came tumbling out fast, tripping over each other.

"You remember, don't you, what happened when I started going to nursery school? When the kids rode their tricycles round and round the driving area, racing one another faster and faster, and I always rode the other way? One day my mother came to pick me up, and the teacher talked to her for ever so long a time. When we got home, Mom asked, 'Honey, how come you don't ride your bike the way the

73

other kids do? It looks like it's so much fun doing it all together.'

" 'I like to go my way,' I said. 'I like it better.'

" 'It's easier to go their way. The teacher says so and I agree with her. She wishes you would just ride along with the others in the same direction they're going. Wouldn't that be nice?'

" 'I won't ride anymore,' I said, 'ever.' "

Rob was smiling. He remembered. "That's when I came into the story," he said. "Knight on a white tricycle, with red wheels and a horn, rides up and saves fair maiden in distress."

"You did love those red wheels, and you blew the horn incessantly. It was incredible luck that just then your family got rid of your nanny and enrolled you in nursery school, and—like a miracle—I asked you to ride counterclockwise and you thought it would be great fun, so we did it together."

"That nursery school teacher nearly went mad," he remembered. "But Amy, that was *so* long ago. It's silly to dwell on it."

"That was just the beginning. After that came ballet lessons, and piano, and singing, and the fiasco with the Girl Scouts. I hated it all. She tried to give me everything she could think of, and I didn't want any of it. The hospital must have made a mistake, Rob. They must have mixed up the babies. I'm a changeling. I can't be her kid. No way." The tears had started again.

"One look in the mirror will kill that theory," he said. "A single look." He dug a big white handkerchief out of his

74

pocket and gave it to me. "Dry your face." He watched silently as I did. When I gave the handkerchief back, he said abruptly, "Look, how would you like to come along with me when I go off to school?"

First I began to giggle. Then I punched him lightly on his chest. "Rob, that's so crazy and noble of you. I bet you would do it, too, if I said yes. You don't know what you're saying. You're my best and oldest friend and I love you, but first of all, the one thing you do not need now is a dependent."

"You would earn your own way, Amy, I know you."

"At what? Minimum wage jobs as waitress or clerk?" I was horrified to hear my mother's arguments coming out of my mouth. But they *were* valid.

"Second of all, Rob, neither of us has tasted life outside of Eastfield yet. Try to imagine all the new experiences that you are going to have, all the new, gorgeous, sexy, brilliant girls you're going to meet when you leave here. Especially when you're a dashing young artist."

"Dashing and poor."

"An irresistible combination. We're too young to decide about each other, Rob. We have to wait and see."

"I'm willing—" he said doggedly, but I went on.

"And third of all, women can't and shouldn't let men save them anymore. I don't mean that the way it sounds, exactly. I mean we have to do things for ourselves, save ourselves, or we'll never be equal. This is a lot more serious than having you ride your tricycle the wrong way to save me, Rob."

"I rode that way because it was more fun. You thought it

up but I loved doing it. *Then* my father stood up for me. He told that nursery school teacher I was a 'rugged individualist' and should be encouraged to go my own way. He said I was right in the New England tradition, the best that built America. Too bad he doesn't feel that way about me anymore." Rob gave me a bear hug. "I love you, Amy Bloomer Hamilton, even though you have a redder nose than W.C. Fields ever did."

"How do you know how red his nose was? You've never seen him in Technicolor."

"I can imagine it."

I was very serious. "Then you have to be able to imagine other kinds of love too."

He took my hand and turned us around so we were starting to walk back toward home. "Anyone who can think that clearly and maturely has no business talking about suicide solving all her problems. No business at all. Don't you worry, Amy. Something wonderful will turn up. By the way, have you seen the opportunities for senior projects? Mr. O posted them yesterday."

"No. Anything good?"

He nodded. "One I'm looking into. Assistant to the art therapist in a mental hospital."

"There *has* to be something for me," I said. "There *has* to be."

There was!

Aged professional quilter seeks apprentice for six week senior project commitment. Room and board, and basic quilting skills offered in exchange for light errands and heavy routine stitching to help complete a quilt for exhibition at a country fair.

No drinkers, smokers, cursers need apply. Send particulars to Box 711, West Hartford, CT.

14

Uncle George kept in close touch. In between his visits to Studio 54, Sardi's, and the Tavern on the Green, and his attendance at all the good plays and the opera, he was scouting around the city for inexpensive ways of printing our school literary magazine. Finally, he called up and said he could get away again, and he wanted to come up and visit. "I'm eager to tell you about this rock-bottom estimate I've gotten for having *Pen & Ink* printed," he said.

I was sure he was eager to see Jessie again too.

"Then there should be an editorial staff meeting," Mom said, "Saturday morning. The editors should help make the decision."

"I'll ask Jan if we can meet at the store," I said. That was our favorite meeting place. When I ran into her at school, she said it would be fine. "I believe my uncle and your mother have something going," I added.

"You believe? He calls her all the time. Like New York was not long distance from here."

"What do you think of Uncle George, Jan?"

She seemed a bit remote. "He's very nice, but"—she bit her lip, and then continued hurriedly—"I really like him. He speaks to me as if he respects my opinion, as if I were an adult; and it's not a pose. He genuinely respects teenagers. How'd that happen?"

"You mean to my mother's brother? To the brother of the woman who said to her seventeen-year-old daughter this morning, 'Wear your heavy coat and be sure you button up. It's a bitterly cold day. And take the wool hat that goes over your ears.' "

Jan smiled. "She means well."

"That is going to be the epitaph they carve on my tombstone: 'Amy Bloomer Hamilton. Passersby, pity her. Her mother meant well.' "

"You take it all too seriously. By the way, you wouldn't believe how much I'm learning in that cram course. It's a long ride to New Haven and a long ride back, a hassle, but they do teach you how to handle questions. I'm not learning any *real* knowledge. I'm learning how to take tests. We do a lot of boring drills that I hate, but I can feel how much it's going to help. You know, the system is just not fair. Poor students who can't raise the money for this kind of course are at a disadvantage. I'm getting a sense of what to expect on the tests, and how to handle it."

"I already know what to expect. Disaster."

"SATs are to disaster as deluges are to floods," Jan said.

"As mad dogs are to rabies," I guessed, "or as murderers are to corpses?"

79

The analogy questions on the exam I took had completely destroyed me, but fooling around this way I could almost enjoy them.

"Okay," I said to Jan, "what's the *but*?"

She looked confused.

"You started to say something before, about Uncle George."

Jan began to shift about the books in her arms. "You won't repeat what I say? Not a word?"

"No. Of course not."

"I like your uncle all right. But I still hope my mom and dad will make up."

"What are the chances?"

"Not good." She shook her head. "Bad."

Uncle George arrived that night. In jeans, Ralph Lauren jeans, true, while the big designer name in Eastfield is Levi, but jeans nonetheless. He had good news. For two hundred dollars our magazine could be handsomely printed using some wonderful new computerized method.

Now all we needed was two hundred dollars.

At ten Saturday morning, Jan, who was hosting the meeting, and a bunch of the other editors including Rob, as well as the interested adults—Mom, Jessie, and Uncle George— and me all sat around in the back of the store. Mostly the other editors ate quantities of sugar cookies and drank cider; they had not known about the problem so they listened carefully. Everyone was immediately enthusiastic about the two-hundred-dollar printing job. Having a fixed sum made it seem possible. It was an amazingly low price because,

Uncle George explained, this was a new, young firm experimenting with new processes. But he had seen a lot of their work, and he'd brought us samples. They were lovely. The problem became how to raise two hundred dollars.

"I know I think in terms of food all the time," Jessie said, a bit hesitantly, "but it does raise money. If there were some unique thing we could cook or bake—all of us—and sell—"

"Yeah, Mom," Jan said, "but you can't make two hundred dollars on a school bake sale. Anyway, by now the kids are saturated with brownies and chocolate chip cookies. You know every school club bakes them, as well as the mothers of every team."

"That's why I said something unique."

"What if we didn't try to sell it here in Eastfield?" Mom asked slowly.

"Where could we sell it?" Rob wondered.

There was a very long silence.

"Well," Mom tried, really searching, "for example, maybe George could find an outlet or two for us in the city. George, your friend who owns the gourmet shop, or maybe some other fancy delicatessen—"

"Yes!" Uncle George said vigorously. "Yes! I could take the goods back with me Sunday night for Monday morning."

"What could we make here that they'd buy in the city and pay a lot for?" I asked.

"It's got to be an indigenous New England food," Jan said.

"SAT word," I teased.

"Right," she said. Then suddenly she jumped up, tremendously excited. "I know!" she screamed. "I have it!"

She had *us*, too, absolutely riveted.

"Mom, those wonderful breads you've been trying for your cookbook."

"Breads?" Uncle George said. "Tell us more."

"There's Apple Corn Bread, Beer Bread, Walnut Honey Bread, and my favorite, Anadama Bread," Jan said.

"I'd be willing to try them all," Bert, our photography editor, said enthusiastically. Bert is really oversized; he's enlisting in the army after graduation, and they'll slim him down, I guess.

Sarah, poetry editor and poet, Oberlin-bound, she hopes, pinched Bert's cheek. "We knew we could count on you, Captain Berty."

"Order," Jan said, amid general laughter. "We better stay with one bread. I vote for Anadama."

"Me too," Sarah said. "The name has a certain fine alliterative quality."

"What a business head!" Bert groaned.

"Listen," Jan went on, "Anadama Bread was invented somewhere in New England by an early colonist, a man whose wife hated to cook, and so she did everything wrong in the kitchen."

"I think I'm descended from Ana," Mom said. "The genealogy sounds about right."

Jan went on, "The story is that she served him plain cornmeal and molasses so often he was driven to baking his own bread. So he kept adding stuff until he came up with this great recipe, and as he baked he went around the kitchen muttering, 'Ana, damn her! Ana, damn her!' That's how the bread got its name."

"Poor fellow," Uncle George said, probably to provoke Mom, who predictably responded, "In my mind it will always be 'Liberation Bread.'"

The vote for Anadama Bread was unanimous. Uncle George went off to call Luigi and easily talked him into considering five sample loaves at $2.50 per loaf.

"We can do the samples here tomorrow morning," Jessie offered, "and if it all works out perhaps the Homemakers Club can do the large-scale baking in school. What do you think, Amy?"

"I think the Club will be a pushover."

"Can we leave that to you?"

"Sure. I'll poll them tonight," I promised.

"Baking in school for outside sale is a pretty irregular activity," Mom said.

Jessie agreed. "Particularly if we need to do it on Sunday mornings."

"I'll have to get Mr. Rooter's permission." Mom was uncertain.

"When we make samples tomorrow, let's make several extra for Mr. Rooter," Alicia, fiction editor, Bryn Mawr-bound, suggested.

"And several extra for us too," Bert added. There were groans and catcalls. "So we can be sure we've got the recipe right." Even more jeering noises, but he just grinned cheerfully.

Mom carried the phone on its long cord in among us and called the Rooter house. We sat mute and hopeful.

Yes, the principal was free tomorrow.

Yes, he could see *Mrs.* Hamilton (he would never give way on the Ms. question) midday, before his dinner, about the literary magazine. Though, he had to say, a weekend conference was highly irregular.

"I'm going to bring you some of the best New England bread you ever ate," Mom promised, "to have with your Sunday dinner."

The voice crackled back at her, making her smile.

"Yes, Mr. Rooter, in a way it *might* be considered a bribe. But not from me. From our students."

The voice was soothed.

Hanging up, Mom bowed to enthusiastic applause.

"I'll wear my highest heels," she resolved. "My Anadama spikes!"

15

Maybe it tells you something about the Homemakers Club to know that they were all home when I phoned them on a Saturday night. Most of our club members don't fit the picture of the typical All-American-High-School-Success. They were, to a woman, delighted with the "bread" idea; it wasn't often that the cooks and the "brains"—writers, poets, artists —in our class got together on a project. Mostly we traveled through high school on parallel tracks, which, we all know, never meet. (SAT math.)

While I was phoning, Uncle George was out with Jessie. I heard him come in late, but Sunday morning was B-for-Breadbaking Day—we wanted perfect samples—and both he and Mom were up early with me. The adults had managed to assemble white flour, cornmeal, molasses, and yeast, as well as the foil pans to bake and ship the breads in. Jessie was Chief Baker and the rest of us measured and mixed and kneaded as needed. Never have breads been more lovingly attended. (Or watched and inhaled: Bert was mesmerized.)

First the flour and salt and cornmeal and yeast were combined. To this was added softened butter and molasses, and then lukewarm water. This mixture was thoroughly beaten, and a bit more flour added, and then the dough was kneaded on floured boards for ten minutes until it was smooth and stretchy. Boy, that takes muscles! Finally the dough was divided into smaller portions and these were put in greased bowls and covered. An hour later each had doubled in bulk. It was amazing to see.

While the dough was rising we greased loaf pans, and when it had risen enough we punched it down (fun!) and divided each in half again. Then we shaped the dough into loaves and put them in the pans. Again it had to stand, covered, until doubled, about forty-five minutes. While it was rising, Rob printed a handsome legend in ye olde style lettering that told the Anadama story. Uncle George was positive the story would sell the bread the first time around. Then the bread would have to sell itself.

How quickly it all went, and how well! Things spilled and got mopped up, and minor errors occurred constantly, but the adults hung around advising and the kids did okay. Even Mom got into the spirit of the occasion, though I knew it was the *Pen & Ink* she cared about more than the bread. The aroma alone was worth the effort; baking bread gives off a scent that rouses hunger in Bert and beast. When the extra breads we'd made for ourselves were cooled a bit, we sliced them up and sat around eating buttered bread, our own brand. I said a private prayer to the legendary Ana. The best thing she ever did was refuse to learn to cook! Our bread was a serendipitous benefit. (SAT word.) The bread was heavenly: crisp-crusted, and soft and smooth inside.

"I think we could ask three dollars a loaf," Uncle George attempted to say, his mouth full.

"Would New Yorkers really pay so much?" Jessie wondered.

"On the Upper East Side of Manhattan? Like that!" Uncle George snapped his fingers easily. "I'll see what Luigi thinks, but I'm willing to bet that three dollars is a good price."

"Wish me luck," Mom said, moving out of her medium-high heels into her highest, which she'd remembered to bring along. Freshly groomed, looking lovely in her gray tweed suit, and double-armed with two of our best breads, she drove off to pay her call on Mr. Rooter.

Our principal is not bad; he's merely timid and a bit old-fashioned. I believe that's why he's principal; he is as advanced at the Eastfield School Board wants their head official to be. He's fair, and I never heard that he was mean to anyone; he would have been a great principal in the Andy Hardy movies. (Mr. O privately agrees; Mr. O is particularly fond of Mr. Rooter because the principal likes movie "classics"; *The Sound of Music* is his favorite classic. No one could dislike a man like that, Mr. O says, and I agree.)

We cleaned up the kitchen as we waited nervously for Mom. If Mr. Rooter said no, it was no bread, no magazine, no nothing. So we swept and scrubbed up, all the while trying to imagine the conversation. More than an hour later we heard Mom coming along long before we saw the car because her hand was playing a triumphal song on the horn.

She had charmed him into saying yes. *Yes!*

"You buttered him up, Doris," Uncle George teased, embracing her, and she freely admitted that she had. It was the "indigenous" recipe that convinced him; Mr. Rooter is a great booster of things New England. We *had* to understand, of course, that we'd be working in an unheated building on Sundays. Mom thought there would be no problem since we'd be baking. The kitchen would warm up rapidly.

Of course, Mr. Rooter also said, he *needn't* tell us that the kitchen would have to be left spotless.

He needn't have told us. Jessie was fanatic about cleanliness.

That night we wrapped the sample breads and packed them with tender loving care, and then Uncle George stowed them in the back of his station wagon. We watched him drive off, and I don't think there was one of us who had a single doubt about those breads.

Some things you *know*. We knew our Anadama Bread would be a success.

Luigi declared them "a steal" at three dollars apiece.

Jessie, amazed, said she had to agree. At three dollars a bread, they were a steal.

Mom was happier than she'd been in months. She almost seemed to have relaxed about her troubles with me. Luigi thought he could sell thirty breads any Monday, so we made big plans.

The next weeks zoomed by. We were all so busy with schoolwork and term papers, plus the Anadama Bread, that personal troubles slipped into the background. First, we had to work for the cause. I had never done anything like this before, never been part of a long-term group effort. I loved it. The editors showed up Sundays along with the Homemakers, and we worked and fooled around and helped one another with the chores. Thirty breads are a lot of dough! During the week when any of us bakers met in passing, the name of the bread, whispered, was enough to cause serious giggles. Other kids thought we were strange. I learned that *doing something* helps chase the blues; and doing something for an outside cause (outside yourself) chases them best of all. There was simply no room in my head for worries about Bennington, or SATs, or my middle name. My mind was elsewhere engaged. We were bread-bakers first, and ourselves second till we'd solved the *Pen & Ink* problem. I couldn't wait for the day Mom could tell Mr. Rooter we had raised enough money to pay for our own printing, and the School Board could all go jump in the lake. Mom wouldn't put it that way, and Mr. Rooter certainly wouldn't put it that way, but in my own mind I liked to put it that way. I loved the idea.

My uncle had become a regular visitor weekends. It seemed to me that George (he asked me not to call him "uncle" anymore, and I did try to remember but it was hard) was spending every free minute he had with Jessie. They walked endlessly, and he'd come back with his eyes bright and happy. I was glad for him but sorry at the same time for Jan. It's bad enough having your father dead the way mine is, but it's even worse to have a nice father and a nice mother, to love them both dearly and to live in continual hope that they'll make up one day and you'll be a whole family again.

In Jan's dream, Uncle George—whom she otherwise liked —was a dangerous intruder.

16

Our front doorbell rang as we were doing the dinner dishes. Mom went to the door.

"Beam me aboard, Captain," a hearty male voice said.

Mom was dissolved in embarrassment. There she was, chairperson of Eastfield High's English department, in old worn khakis and a *Star Trek* T-shirt I had bought for her. And, on her feet, Nikes. No psychological advantage whatsoever.

"You look terrific, Doris," Mr. O said, coming in. "You look about fifteen years old."

"You Vulcans have no sense of human age," Mom said. "Why didn't you put the phone receiver to your pointed ear and call me first?"

"Mom!" I congratulated her. She periodically surprises me with her knowledge of pop culture because she's always putting it down.

"If I'd phoned, you might have set up a force field and kept me away. I had to see you two tonight."

"Well—" Grudgingly, she let him in; and grudgingly, she let him sit down; and grudgingly, she offered him a cup of tea. Graciously, he accepted every offer and took no notice of her manner at all.

I was about to make a swift disappearance upstairs when he said, "We need you here, Amy B, so please stick around. This visit mostly concerns you."

"Oh?" Mom was suddenly a lot more interested.

I came in and sat down across from him.

"It would seem that Amy has found a senior project that is absolutely perfect for her. The odd thing about it is"—he reached into his back pocket and drew forth a folded letter on lilac notepaper—"it's working with *my* great-aunt."

I gasped.

"Yes?" said Mom. She could make *yes* sound just like *no*.

"Amy didn't know about her being my aunt when she applied," he continued. "She answered a senior project ad. We never post names. I just got this inquiry from Aunt Edna today."

"Whoa. Back up a little. What kind of senior project?" Mom asked. "What kind of working with your aunt?"

"Making quilts."

"Quilts?" Mom looked stunned.

"Yes," I said, "quilts."

"You mean patchwork quilts?"

He nodded. "This is my paternal aunt, a very old lady, who quilts for a living and who cannot manage by herself too well anymore. She lives in West Hartford."

Mom did not look enthusiastic.

"No one knows how old she is because she won't tell. She's very feisty and independent. However, her eyesight is not so good anymore and she's not as quick as she'd like to be. On bad days she can't go to the store, so she's sort of isolated. Amy, she's prepared to offer six weeks working with her as her general assistant, helping her along with the quilt she's getting ready for the Independence Day Fair, where she's exhibited for more than forty years. She used to do every stitch herself, but these last years it's gotten to be too much for her. If you like the work and the two of you get on together, she'd be glad to have you as an apprentice for a year, at a salary. Not huge, but fair. She earns enough on her quilts to be able to do that comfortably."

"Next year is out of the ques—" Mom started.

I didn't give her a chance to finish. "Yes!" I said. "Yes, yes, yes, yes, yes! For the senior project, and if she wants me for the whole year. Yes!"

"You two didn't cook this up behind my back?" Mom asked, and then she had the grace to be embarrassed. "I didn't mean that, Jim—and Amy—I apologize."

"I'll get your tea for you, Mr. O," I offered, and hurried into the safety of the kitchen, leaving the two of them to work things out.

That must have been *some* dialogue in sign language because I didn't hear a sound. I kept the gas flame low so it took a very long time for the kettle to whistle. I was in no hurry to return to the living room. Finally, I didn't feel I could stall any longer. I had to bring him his tea.

"Thank you," he said. "Do sit down with us now."

93

I glanced at them as I sat next to Mom on the couch. She was sitting there sort of limp while Mr. O sat up straight facing us on the deacon's bench. He stirred his tea, and sipped. "Doris, you have Greek handmade rugs," he said, obviously continuing what must have been a whispered argument, "and a Mexican weaving on your wall that you admire enormously."

"Because they're beautiful."

"So is American handicraft. Don't be such an utter snob. You never used to be so stuffy. You've been teaching small-town high school too long. The women who do this kind of work are artists." He sipped again. "Let's put it to the person who counts most," he suggested. "Amy, how do you feel about Aunt Edna's proposition?"

"It's sensational. I'd love it. I'd love to learn to quilt, and I'm sure I'd enjoy being apprenticed to your aunt. Is she a movie fan too?"

He laughed. "Aunt Edna? She's never had time for movies. What she likes to do best is work with her hands, and that's what she does. She embroiders. She makes lace. She's done some remarkable needlepoint. She says movies are for idlers like me."

Even Mom had to smile at that because Mr. O works harder than anyone else at school.

"She does have a radio," he said. "And another wonderful entertainment that I won't tell you about. Let it be a surprise."

"And what about college?" Mom asked, her voice strained.

"I don't know, Mom. But for my senior project, at least,

94

it's a sensational opportunity. Thank you, Mr. O, for coming here tonight. Thank you for saving my life."

"My pleasure," he said. "You seem to have written a good letter of application. Aunt Edna was much taken with it."

"And if Amy *likes* quilting," Mom spoke, unhappy but, at least, not hysterical, "is that to be her profession, her calling? Is she to make a living today out of quilting?"

Mr. O looked at her steadily. "She could. There's a great demand for lovely quilts. My aunt can't possibly do them fast enough for all the orders she gets. But Amy may want to do many things. She should do whatever appeals to her and is productive, whatever makes her happy."

"Please, Mom," I begged, "please say yes. For the senior project, at least." She would have to sign the senior project contract.

She looked at Mr. O.

"Say yes, Doris," he urged quietly. "You won't be sorry."

"Yes," she said, at last, "though I probably *will* be sorry."

I leaned over and hugged her. I knew it took a lot for her to say yes.

"You'll have to go over to West Hartford for an interview," Mr. O reminded me. "You don't have the placement until Aunt Edna interviews you and approves."

"I'll go," I said, "and I'll get it. Your Aunt will like me. In fact, she'll love me. Now I'm going to run over and tell Jan." I was out the door and away very fast. This news could not keep.

. . .

Jan was delighted for me. "I hope you get it," she said. "Be smooth. Be charming. Be Miss Quilter, USA, in every way."

I raised a shoulder and struck an attractive pose, one hip jutting crazily while with my hands I pretended to thread an invisible needle.

Jan had just finished working out her own project. The Infant Day-Care Center of St. John's Church had hired her (at the minimum wage) to work with very tiny babies.

"Since I am thinking about early childhood education and teaching," she said, "it's a terrific chance. And I'll make some money. That SAT course really cleaned me out."

"That's *very very* early childhood education, Jan. Mostly you'll probably be changing diapers."

"I don't mind. I love little babies."

"Will you still feel that way afterward?"

"Who knows? But that's what these senior projects are supposed to be for. To give us chances to try things. Since I plan to have six or eight children of my own, this will probably be a good experience."

"*Six* or *eight*?"

"Yeah. A few biological and the rest adopted."

"Boy, you're ambitious. You're looking so far ahead. I only want to learn how to make quilts. Gorgeous, prize-winning quilts."

"You can make quilts for my babies' beds."

"I can earn a living on your family alone if you have all those kids."

"I'll try to live in Alaska or some other cold place, Amy. Then we'll need lots of quilts."

"I don't know about all those kids," I said. "Sometimes kids are hard to take."

"Don't you like kids?"

"I suppose," I said, "but you know what W.C. Fields said when he was asked that question. He said, 'I do. If they're properly cooked.'"

"Ugh. Mr. O must be hanging around your house. I can tell."

I tried to look astonished. "How?"

17

On Sunday I took the Greyhound bus to West Hartford for my interview. I had arranged it by phone "after church and lunch," two o'clock sharp. I was dressed as conservatively and nicely as I could be: dark blue plaid, pleated skirt, white man-tailored shirt, loafers, and nylons. My usually loose long hair was cinched in a neat ponytail.

I rang the bell, and the door of the shabby white clapboard house was opened briskly a moment later.

"Ms. O'Brien? I'm Amy Hamilton."

"Not Ms. Miss. I didn't marry on principle and I want that noted." She was a firecracker. "I had plenty of chances but they were either fools or they took alcohol so I chose to remain Miss O'Brien." She was small and spare, with lively blue eyes much like her great-nephew's, and startling white eyebrows and lashes. Also the same soft abundant white hair, hers done up in a bun on her head; she looked beautifully frosted. Dressed in black silk, a cameo brooch at her neck, Miss Edna O'Brien was a graceful step back to the turn of the century. She led me into the living room crowded with handsome, old-fashioned furniture: a couch and chairs with elegantly turned legs and plush upholstery, a massive table with a raffia sewing basket on it, and a sideboard that covered an entire wall. Against the other wall was an incredibly old dollhouse, a white clapboard miniature of the house we were in. I knew at once that it was the wonderful entertainment Mr. O had hinted at. She headed for the dollhouse, beckoning me over to it.

"This is mine," she said. "My oldest brother made it for me when I was five years old. He's dead many years now, but this dollhouse keeps him alive for me. I love it."

"I can see why."

"I'll share it with you while you are here, Amy, if you decide to come."

I had already decided.

The dollhouse was fully furnished, curtained, rugged, and populated with a family of exquisitely dressed tiny dolls with cloth bodies and hand-painted china faces and china limbs.

"I make new things for the dollhouse all the time," she said. "Often classes of schoolchildren come here to see it, and I tell them about it. You might help me with that too." Taking my hand in her small, cool hand, she led me over to the couch and seated me. Then she sat down directly across from me in a straight-backed plush chair fringed with tiny tassels.

"Ready?" she asked me. "I was impressed with your note. It was direct, and sincere, and neat. And I must tell you in all honesty, it was the only inquiry I got. So—why quilting? In the 1980s why do you want to learn quilting? By the way, I love your name. I've always admired Amelia Bloomer. Your name was one of the reasons I wrote to Jim at once and asked him to send you along."

"Well"—I started brilliantly—"well, you see, I'm about to graduate from high school and I don't know what I want to do. I like to sew, and, in general, I enjoy working with my hands. I knit and I crochet. I thought I'd like to learn to quilt. I think patchwork quilts are really neat."

"Neat," she repeated, nodding.

"Yes," I said. "Then, later on, I might learn to weave. There are so many wonderful things to learn, and I was looking for a place to begin. When I saw your note posted outside Mr. O's office, I thought you'd be the person to begin with. So I wrote to you."

Her head was bobbing encouragingly as I spoke.

"Jim is a sweetie," she said.

I had to smile. That's exactly what he is.

"He's my favorite great-nephew. His grandfather built my dollhouse. He once considered becoming a man of the cloth, you know, but he had no real calling. He also once considered marrying your mother, but she was foolish. She turned him down. He's a man in a million. Never tell him I said so. He's peculiar enough with all that movie nonsense. We can't turn his head."

I grinned. It was fun to hear her talk about my college adviser that way. As if he were a young child.

Miss O'Brien noted the grin and read my mind. "I say

what I think, Amy. I'm a woman of strong opinions. Some might even say strong and unbalanced opinions, but I don't care what anyone says. I'm old enough to be free to say anything I choose. And I'll tell you something." She looked at me slyly. "I've always been old enough."

From the sewing basket on the table she took a needle and thread and four two-inch cotton cloth squares. "Seam these together," she said, "in a block."

I tried for tiny stitches; there was nothing to it. Miss O'Brien put on pink plastic-rimmed glasses and inspected my stitches. "Neat," she said. There was a long silence while she mulled things over, all the while staring straight at me. "We'll see," she said at last. "Come."

She rose and I followed her. We went through the hall with its wooden staircase to a door opposite the living room. "I work in the sunroom," she said, throwing open the door. The room was huge and light, crammed full of bolts of fabric and paper patterns and bags of cloth scraps; occupying a huge area was a wood frame about eight feet long on which a gorgeous quilt was stretched. The quilt had a white background and interlinking large rings made up of bright varied patterns. The afternoon light picked up all the colors beautifully.

"It's lovely," I said.

"The pattern is called 'Double Wedding Ring'; it's very old." She glanced around her workroom fondly. "I do love color," she said. "Color is the Lord's gift to the eyes. We won't go into the workroom today. I keep Sunday as a rest day. If I walked in, I'd be sorely tempted."

"You love quilting that much?"

"Even more, child. Even more. It's the reason I live. It's the reason I live happily. I've been doing it for almost seventy years. Started when I was a very small child." She closed the door, and, holding on to the knob, she spoke very seriously.

"Before we go any further I have to say to you that the work you'll be doing with me for the next few weeks is not true quilting. I don't want you coming here under false pretenses. True quilting means starting with scraps, choosing your own pattern, cutting the pieces to shape, and then seaming them together side to side, like making a cloth mosaic. Then the quilt gets put together, a plain underside of percale or muslin, a layer of cotton batting, and then the patchwork top. But I've already done all the beginning steps on this Double Wedding Ring and what's left now is the stitching together. I always did every single stitch in my quilts by my own hand, but these last years I've had trouble. I can't possibly finish this one by July fourth, not alone I can't, so I need help. Will you find it boring?"

"I don't think so."

She pulled her earlobe. Then a wicked smile lit up her lined face. "I can start you on a quilt of your own in your spare time. I can teach you other things evenings."

"I'd really like that."

"And how to make things for the dollhouse too," she promised. "Beautiful miniatures. The clothing gets shabby because the children love to handle the dolls."

We seemed to be in absolute agreement.

102

"Let me show you where you will sleep," she said, leading me up the steep wooden stairs to a small room with two dormer windows. There was old-fashioned flowered wallpaper on the walls, cream-colored with tiny bouquets of forget-me-nots, a huge lumpy bed, and a green dresser that looked a little wobbly on its legs. In one corner, next to an end table with a hurricane lamp on it, stood an overstuffed chair.

"We'll share the bathroom," she said. "This house has only one. I think I had better warn you that it has a tub and no shower." She said that as if it were somehow very significant.

"That's okay," I said. "I like baths."

"Good girl. Last year a college sent me a girl who was dying to learn how to quilt right up until the minute she saw the old bathtub. Then she left."

"I guess she wasn't dying to learn how to quilt."

"No. She was dying to take showers. Amy, I think you should also know that I don't own a television set. On principle. I believe in real life, not images. I save my eyes for quilting."

"Mr. O told me."

"That man talks a lot." She smiled fondly. Slowly, she led the way back downstairs and into the living room again. "Well then, it's all settled. Why don't you bring your things and move in right after Easter, and we'll start working together. I work every day except Sunday, using as many of the good light hours as possible. That means the early hours of the day. You don't have to work all that time." She paused, as if her statement had been a question.

"Miss O'Brien," I said, "I appreciate this wonderful opportunity."

She shook her head. "No, no. I am getting a free apprentice, you know. An apprentice that I need very badly. So you've got no reason to think you won't be earning your keep. That and more."

I got up to go, and she rose as well.

"Child," she said, "it will be a great pleasure for me to have you here. You'll be company as well as help for me. And, if you really like quilting, Jim says you might want to come back for a while next autumn. But we'll wait to see how the senior project trial time goes."

"Yes," I said.

She took my hand and squeezed it. "I'll pray that it will work out well for both of us. I do like young people, and I'd love to share the dollhouse. So I look forward to having you here with me."

I skipped all the way to the bus station, feeling about seven years old.

I couldn't remember the last time I'd skipped anywhere, or the last time I'd been so happy. I'd arranged it! Miss O'Brien and her dollhouse were another life, a more gracious time for me to wander in for a bit. They were the best of the past till I dared the future.

18

I was in the midst of putting together a new Indian Pudding recipe that Jessie had just unearthed (there are many such recipes, and she wanted to use the best one in her book), when Dr. Burton phoned and asked if he might stop by and see me. Just he, not Mrs. Burton, and not Rob. Mom was about to take off for the attic when the call came. Both of us were surprised, she more than I. "Dr. Burton wants to see you? What about?"

"Not about Indian Pudding. Pocahontas never had such interruptions, that's for sure." I hate to be sidetracked when I'm trying something new. It's so easy to spoil a dish. Cooking's got to be done with care.

"I think I know what this is about, Mom. Rob and his senior project. Rob and college."

"I think he should give premed a chance," Mom said.

"Now how did I know you would think that?"

"It's a wonderful opportunity." She disregarded my comment.

"He doesn't have a vocation," I said. "Not for medicine."

"That's a nineteenth-century word. You hardly hear it these days."

"SAT word," I said.

She looked at me curiously. "How does he know yet what he has?"

I laughed. "Come on, Mom. You *know* when you have a vocation."

"He can't be sure yet," she said. "He's too young."

"He knows he wants to study art. He wants to learn everything there is to know about painting and sculpture. *That's* a vocation."

Mom sighed. "He'll never make a living."

"How can you say that? The art department thinks he's sensational. You know how good his drawings are for the magazine. You've said yourself that some of them seem 'inspired.'"

"He is good. But ours is a high school magazine, Amy. It's not the Museum of Modern Art. There are millions of talented people out there competing with one another."

"It's always been that way, Mom. He has faith in himself. When you're young you're entitled to try. That's all he wants to do."

"And if he fails? What then? What his father is trying to do is guarantee him a good life. He's trying to protect Rob against failure."

"And against real success, the success that he might have doing what he wants to do."

Mom took up her cup of tea and went off. Even she was getting tired of futile conversations.

There was no point in going on with the cooking till afterward.

I paged through the new *Seventeen* magazine till the doorbell rang. I opened the door to Dr. Burton—tall, rangy, weary-looking. Suddenly, our parents were all looking old. I showed him into our living room, but he refused to sit down.

"I've come for some help, Amy," he started. "You know, of course, about Yale accepting Rob. And you know about this insanity of his: art instead of medicine?"

I nodded.

"And what do you think?"

I was silent.

"What shall I do with him?"

"Let him do what he wants to, Dr. Burton," I said, with more courage than I knew I had.

"Ah?" he said, looking at me sharply. "That's the problem. He doesn't really know what he wants to do. He *thinks* he knows. He *thinks* he wants to be an artist, but I know better. Medicine is an exalted career, a service career as well as a remunerative profession. Once he was in it he'd find beauty and pleasure and plenty of challenge."

"Art is an important career too," I said boldly. "It provides beauty to a world that needs it."

"No sensible person would compare the two," he said quickly.

"Thank you."

"I didn't mean it personally, of course, Amy."

I was silent.

"Amy?"

"I don't know what to say to you," I began quietly. "Dr. Burton, you remember my mother's pledge?"

"I could never forget it. Bennington College."

"I'm not going there. I'm not going to college at all. I'm going off to learn quilting."

"Quilting?" He pronounced it as though he were afraid it would burn his mouth.

"Yes."

"Why quilting?"

"It's a skill I admire, and I'm good with my hands. So I'm going to learn how to do it."

"Your mother will not be able to support you forever, you know."

"I don't expect her to support me. Quilts sell for good prices."

"Quilts," he said to himself. "Quilts! Where do you children get your ideas?" He shook his head. "I had hoped that you would talk to Rob for me, Amy."

"It wouldn't do any good even if I were willing. He's made up his mind."

Dr. Burton looked at me suspiciously. "Have you been encouraging him to do this? Are you the leader as you were with the tricycles?"

"That time you backed him up. He remembers how you encouraged him to be an individualist."

"He was a young child and I didn't want his character squashed by stupid and pedantic rules."

"But Dr. Burton, he's that same young child grown up!"

"Not quite." He studied me intently. "*Have* you been encouraging him to do this?" It was not a question; it was an accusation.

"Dr. Burton, he didn't need me. The art department says he's a remarkable student, one of the best they've ever had. Everyone thinks he's very talented, everyone except you."

"I think he's talented. I like Robert's work exceedingly. Doctors appreciate beauty too, you know. Robert can always be a Sunday painter. Like Winston Churchill. Many great men were doctors as well as practitioners of the various arts. William Carlos Williams was a full-time doctor and a poet over in Paterson, New Jersey; and then there was Somerset Maugham, and Chekhov, and, of course, John Keats. Rob can do his art as an avocation."

"Maugham and Chekhov and Keats didn't do their art as hobbies," I said. "They left medicine."

He seemed surprised and somewhat annoyed by this information, which he probably heard as impertinence. Contradiction, at least.

"Because my mother teaches literature and talks about writers," I explained, "I know about them."

He closed his eyes and pressed them with his fingertips. "I can't figure out what went wrong. Three generations of Burtons have studied medicine at Yale. Studied it with zeal. I have two capable sons: one ends up a baseball player and the other wants to be a dilettante."

109

"An artist," I insisted. "He's serious about it. He wants a chance to go his own way."

"And if it happens to be the wrong way?"

"He'll have to go back and start all over again with something else."

The doorbell rang and rang. I went and opened it to a furious Rob, his face red, his hair wild, his horn-rims slipping down on his nose. He pushed past me to confront his father. "Mom told me you were here," he said angrily.

"She should not have said anything."

"Whatever you're trying to do, you're too late. I've signed up to do my senior project at a hospital, all right, but it's the State Psychiatric Hospital. I'll be assisting in art therapy, doing exactly what I'd hoped to do."

"I didn't sign—" Dr. Burton started, and then he must have realized that his wife had signed the parental consent slip.

"Congratulations, Rob," I said.

He didn't take any notice. His anger with his father was too great, too overwhelming.

If only he had just turned around and left then, just turned around and walked out. But he didn't.

"Why did you have to come here?" he demanded of his father.

"I wanted to speak to Amy."

"What has she to do with it?"

"She's your friend."

"So?"

"I just thought I would sound her out."

110

"You came to bully her," Rob accused. "You probably came to blame her too. You think I can't do anything independently, on my own. Well, she had nothing to do with my decision. Absolutely nothing. She's got enough troubles of her own. Why didn't you just leave her alone? Why pick on a girl?" He stood between his father and me as though I were especially fragile or vulnerable and he had to shield me.

"I can take care of myself, Rob," I said hotly. "Honest, I was doing fine."

"You certainly were, young lady." Dr. Burton's tone was far from admiring. "Thank you for your time. Come along, Robert. I sense that we are both quite unwelcome here at this time."

Rob looked at me for a signal to stay, but I was miffed. He thought I was so weak that I needed to be saved from his father. From his father's *words!* When would the world, the people I loved in it, particularly, recognize that I was a competent adult?

"Go home with your father, Rob," I said. "I have to finish this Indian Pudding I started. Squaw's work."

He knew me so well, he understood. "I'll talk to you," he said.

We left it at that.

19

Uncle George drove down unexpectedly. We had enough *Pen & Ink* money, so the visit was not business, just pure pleasure. He was out late Saturday night with Jessie. I was asleep when he came in.

Sunday morning I got up early and wandered into the kitchen, and there he was already at the table, drinking coffee and looking wretched. I mean beat. Mom wouldn't be conscious for hours so I knew I'd have to find out what was wrong myself.

"You sick?" I asked. Usually he kept his New York habits —that is, when we weren't on a bread-baking crusade: he slept as late as possible and then lay around in pajamas as long as possible. That seemed to be the New York idea of the perfect Sunday morning. Mom had picked it up from him. "Why you up so early?"

He shrugged.

I poured myself some orange juice and went to sit across

from him. One thing he is is a talker; I had never seen him mute the way he was now.

"Trouble?" I asked.

"You might say that."

"May I know about it?"

He hesitated. Took a sip of his coffee. Sighed. "You'll know soon enough. Jessie and her husband are going to give their marriage another try."

"I'm sorry for you, Uncle George."

"Me too," he said. "Me too. They're really doing it for Jan. She wants them back together again," he said distantly. Then he corrected himself, abruptly. "No. I'm being dishonest. It's Jessie who wants to try again. She's not comfortable with the separation, and she'd probably be even more unhappy with a divorce. She still loves him. That's why she's never taken any legal steps. Jan is just one part of it all. Anyway, Mike Campbell has landed a job, at last, at a small community college way out in the sticks in Massachusetts."

"Sociology?" I asked.

"Believe it or not. He hung on long enough and he got his job in sociology. You've got to give the man credit for tenacity. It's not a first-rate school, but he'll manage there."

"I'm sorry for you, Uncle George, but I'm glad for them. Jan will be so happy! And maybe there'll be some money for college."

"In a way I'm glad for them too. Only, just now, I feel sorrier for me. No doubt it will pass." He looked past me out the large kitchen window at the bird feeder where two robins were busy pecking seeds. "It could have been very nice," he sighed. "Jessie is a rare person besides being an incredible cook."

I came around and gave him a kiss on the cheek.

"Don't worry, kid. I'll live through it. I've been disappointed before. Maybe I'm best off with Chiara. She's really an impressive woman. And fun."

"Can she cook?"

"Her specialties are imaginative salads: mushrooms, watercress, artichokes, avocadoes. The works."

"Can't she make anything but salads?"

"Amy, if you want to be stylish you have to make sacrifices. Chiara is a strong, self-made woman. She cares about style; she's gorgeous."

"I think you're making her up," I teased him. "Why don't you bring her along some weekend so we can meet her?"

"I just might," he said, "when all of this has faded a little. She'd like to meet my family, I know."

"Promise? Bring her when I'm back here for the summer. After graduation."

"I promise." He smiled. "I'll be just fine. Jessie was right; I am a city mouse at heart."

"I wonder what I am, Uncle George."

"Kid, you've got the whole rest of your life to make discoveries about yourself. And you will, you will. Now, how would you like to collaborate with me on a mighty breakfast? Let's surprise your mother."

"Yes," I said, "cheese omelets, and we'll serve her hers in bed. Toast, marmalade, and *café au lait* the way she loves it."

"We'll make her feel like a Sybarite," he promised, heading for the refrigerator.

"*Sybarite*: one who loves luxury and pleasure."

Uncle George was amused. "You learned some good words," he said. "See, those tests aren't all bad."

The face I made could have curdled the milk.

20

"My mother was a quilter," Miss O'Brien started. "Her own mother had taught her, and she came to her marriage with her own handmade quilts. I slept under one, a Rose of Sharon, all through my childhood.

"I was the youngest of three sisters, and I used to watch the others piecing and play with the scraps of cloth. I was horribly jealous of my sisters because they got to do this grown-up work. When I was six, right smack on my birthday as an extra present, Mother said, 'Come help with a straight-line quilt.' She was very kind and patient, showing me again and again how to keep my stitches small and in straight rows. It was women's work we were doing—me being six years old —and we did it all together. What a pleasure it was.

"Then my father came in for his tea, and he looked at my stitches and he said to Mother, loud so I and everybody could hear, 'Them's basting stitches Edna is putting in. You're just going to have to take them all out or your quilt'll be spoilt.' He took great pride in Mother's quilts, and well he might.

" 'You go 'long and have your tea,' Mother told him, 'you don't know beans about quiltin'. Edna is just beginning on her first quilt and she's doing mighty fine work. Mighty fine. I've known girls ten years old couldn't do stitches like those.'

"Well, I kept at it, and I tried very hard to make my stitches smaller and smaller so next time Father looked he would hardly be able to see them at all, and he'd have to say what a good sewer I was, but he never did look a second time. I think that was when I first realized that you can't count on men. Years later I asked Mother if she had secretly ripped out those first big stitches. They really were horse-blanket stitches, you know. But she kissed me and laughed and said, 'No, child. Only God creates perfect things. I kept your stitches for that, and because they reminded me of a happy family day.' She really believed it was bad luck to try for perfection, so she always put a slight flaw in each quilt. I do it too; one patch is always a little off. Just custom. To remind myself of her.

"I've been quilting ever since then, off and on, all my life. Oh, I tried other occupations, but I didn't care for them. I was a cashier in a clothing shop and a clerk in a large law office. There was nothing to show for my labor, afterward. I worked and got paid, and then the money was spent. When I quilt, even when I sell the quilt and never see it or its owner again, it's still out there and it gives someone warmth, and comfort, and real pleasure.

117

"Quilting is a gift. When God gives you a gift you don't turn it aside. You use it and enjoy it." She got up and came around to where I was stitching (it was fairly simple work putting the quilt together, since she had done all the intricate sewing before I ever appeared on the scene), and she looked closely at my work. "Delicate," she said, and patted my shoulder encouragingly, "nice and neat. You might have the gift, Amy. We'll have to see."

During the days I quilted on her quilt and during the evenings she began to teach me the basics: how to use the template, the master copy of the shape to be used for the patches; how to cut lining and interlining; how to work out simple patterns; all the various stitches.

"Mother's quilts were made up of scraps from old clothes," she said, "so that if there was a dress I loved, I had it for years afterward in a quilt. But for my quilts I use only cotton cloth and all of it new fabric because I sell my quilts and they need to be strong. Old cloth is sometimes too worn to give good service. Other quilters use various fabrics, but I put my trust in cotton. I think it's very beautiful."

I came to love cotton as much as she did.

Time passed very quickly. I read some, and walked, and worked on things for the dollhouse. I made a tiny red-tissue kite for a boy doll, and a pink dress with white pantaloons underneath for an older girl doll. The furnishings were exquisite: miniature stuffed furniture and a rocking chair, an entire old-fashioned kitchen with a pump sink and coal stove, china dishes, and food shaped and painted to look real—bread, roast beef, fruits, potatoes. There were tiny metal utensils—a colander and a spatula, and the like. It was a little girl's dream and a big girl's dream too. Sometimes teachers brought their classes of young children to see the dollhouse, and then we'd all have such a good time together. The children were allowed to hold the dolls and examine the dollhouse carefully. Nothing had ever been stolen and a very few things had been broken over the years; the children were remarkably careful.

Daily, I ran errands for Miss Edna. (She asked me to call her that.) Everyone in the neighborhood knew her, and neighbors often stopped me to ask, "How's Miss Edna? Will the quilt be done in time?" Each year she kept the pattern of her new quilt a secret until the day of the Fair; several nosy women tried to ferret information out of me, but Miss Edna had coached me carefully to "look stupid and say little." I loved doing it.

Whenever I felt in the mood to, I did some cooking. Otherwise, oddly, Miss Edna turned out to be a takeout person like my own mother. She'd eat anything quick and easy to prepare, or, better yet, to bring in: barbecued chicken, hamburgers, pizzas. Though she had no TV she was an enthusiastic consumer of TV dinners.

"Got to get up and use the dawn's early light," she'd say, "and by the time the light is gone, I'm tired and I don't fancy cooking. I felt the same way fifty years ago so it hasn't to do with my age." She loved to eat though, and it was a pleasure to cook for her and see how much she could finish.

"Maybe that's why no man married me, in the end," she said. "I scared them all away with my appetite. Mother used

119

to tell us girls, 'At parties, just nibble. Just pick at the food.' But I always finished everything in sight."

I really grew to love and admire her. Oh, she was peppery —not with me because I didn't cross her, but when the sewing store where she bought her supplies overcharged me twenty cents on each of a dozen spools of number five white mercerized cotton thread, she put on her hat (which had wonderful red felt cherries on it, as well as a small dotted swiss veil), and took me by the arm and insisted on going down there to scold them. It was impressive to watch her and to listen to her.

Miss Edna had the clerk and the owner begging her forgiveness. Begging, I swear. It had been an honest error, I thought, but she disagreed. She believed that because I was a new face come to shop there, it must have been done intentionally. One of her favorite topics was how honest shopkeepers *used* to be. Well! After that interview it was perfectly safe to send me to that store for any purchases; the owner himself handled my orders.

So the days passed, quietly but not dully.

Rob wrote. He apologized for thinking I couldn't manage with his father. *I guess I keep seeing that sad little girl in kindergarten,* he wrote. *Forgive me.* He was having a very interesting time assisting patients in art therapy. In the evenings he sketched patients' portraits, giving the sketches to the models whenever they wanted them. Some tore them up immediately. A few loved them and saved them. Many were simply not interested in them afterward. They were not interested in anything external, Rob said. Having all these live models was a wonderful opportunity. In high school sketch class the best live model they could come up with was a duck!

Jan was busy with the babies in the day-care center. Turned out she didn't mind the diaper bit a bit. The focus of her letters was not really on her senior project; it was on her mother and father, who were together now in Eastfield trying to wind things up so they could move to their new home in rural Massachusetts. This time they were planning to live on a farm! I was sorry to think of their moving, but Jan was going away to college anyway in the fall, and I would be away, too, quilting. We would keep in touch.

Mom wrote often and I wrote to her. She missed me but she was busy and fine. When *Pen & Ink* came out she surprised me with a visit, personally coming to deliver my copy to West Hartford one bright morning. The doorbell rang and there she stood in a pretty blue-flowered dress and her highest-heeled pumps.

"Miss Edna, it's my mother! Mom, this is Miss Edna O'Brien."

Miss Edna was most cordial. "Welcome," she said. "You have a lovely and gifted daughter."

Gifted!

"You should have come on a Sunday when we are idle and can entertain you better, but do come into our workroom and keep us company while we stitch. Words make needles fly. The old quilting bees were very efficient, you know. The gossip flew and the needles flew." She looked my mother over. "You're a very good-looking woman," she said.

My mother smiled and blushed deeply.

Any conversation that starts off that way has got to be good. And this one was.

Mom stayed two hours, sitting with us in the workroom. Miss Edna and I sewed while we talked, except for a short break for tea and chocolate marshmallow cookies, Miss Edna's favorites.

Mom couldn't stop raving about the Double Wedding Ring quilt. "It's truly beautiful," she said. "It's almost too beautiful to use."

"It's a traditional pattern," Miss Edna said, "and it's quite durable. You can't wear one of these out."

Mom was still skeptical about quilting as a means to earn a living, and—even more—about it as an acceptable profession, but the quality of the quilt could not be denied. She loved beautiful things, so she had to love what we were creating.

"Look at Amy's stitches," Miss Edna said. "They're so fine I can't hardly tell which are hers and which are mine anymore."

It was my turn to blush with joy.

Over tea, we paged through the *Pen & Ink*. Uncle George's bargain printing method had proved to be terrific. The magazine was handsome and Mom was filled with optimism. She kept saying she was sure Eastfield High would win some big prize in the Columbia University national contest for high school magazines. "Then the School Board will realize the error of its ways. No athletic team of ours ever won very much, and all the extracurricular money gets spent on them.

If our magazine wins a prize, things have to be different next year. They'll be so proud of *Pen & Ink* they'll be glad to fund it." She had written those happy thoughts to Uncle George while the magazine was still on press because I had a note from him cautioning me not to spoil her daydreams. *Let her enjoy the magazine when it comes out,* he wrote. *Football will get the money again next year, but that's the way things are. Time enough to suffer then.* Meanwhile he was off on a wine-tasting tour of the French chateau country.

"I've been feeling so happy about the magazine," Mom said. "I'm full of energy. I'm back at my writing these days."

When she took her leave, she was truly gracious to Miss Edna. "I'm glad Amy is here," she said, "and I'm glad she's learning so much from you. I've had my doubts. I still do about quilting as a livelihood, but I can see that this is wonderful for her."

Miss Edna offered her hand. "Life is long and full of choices," she said. "This is only a very early one for Amy."

Mom blew me a kiss and then went tapping off on those heels.

"Your mother should wear more comfortable shoes," Miss Edna said. "Why ever would she want to be handicapped by those stilts?"

"Psychological advantage," I said. "Taller people dominate."

Miss Edna snorted. "Claptrap! Let's get back to our sewing."

21

And so, before I knew it, my time was almost up.

I had started on a quilt in earth colors, browns and oranges and tans, using a simple hexagonal pattern. It was to be a gift for Mom. I didn't want to use ordinary stitching. I wanted this quilt to be special.

Miss Edna had taught me an alternate way of quilting that I liked a lot, Tied quilting, in which the three basic layers of top, batting, and backing are held together by individual separate stitches that are tied and knotted, instead of by continuous rows of stitchery. I got a brilliant idea.

"Miss Edna, could I buy some beautiful beads and tie one into each stitch?"

At first, she wasn't enthused. Not that it had never been done before. It had. But, for her, patchwork offered beauty enough.

"But I'm using plain cloth," I argued, "no fancy patterns, just earth colors. Beads would really dress the quilt up."

She put on her wonderful fruity hat once again, and we

ventured downtown. There, in Andy Crafts, a new art supply store, the young proprietor, Andy (he looked about twenty; he was amazingly blond and handsome), showed us a basketful of unpolished sandalwood beads, beautiful and fragrant.

"Would they work on a quilt?" I wondered.

"Why not? I use them in making necklaces and earrings," he said. "They're lovely."

"I agree, young man," Miss Edna said. "They'll do beautifully."

We bought a quantity of them. "Let me know how they work out on your quilt," Andy said, as he wrapped them. "In fact, I'd like to see the quilt." He smiled, and I had good vibes. Here was a friend in the offing. "We have a crafts group that meets here Wednesday nights," he said. "You're invited."

"I'd love to," I said wistfully, "but I'm going away for a while."

"Well then, when you come back."

The very first Wednesday, I resolved. *Maybe I can arrange to come back on a Wednesday.*

"We will name this wooden-bead stitch after you," Miss Edna said, as we made our way home. "That's the way stitches get named, after the first person who creates them in her own new way."

"Under no circumstances do I want to be responsible for a stitch named Amelia Bloomer Hamilton! Or even just Hamilton, though that's not quite as bad." I considered it as we walked along. "Could I call it the 'Bennington Stitch' in memory of another stitch a long time ago?"

"It's your stitch, girl. Call it whatever you like."

And then it was time to leave.

Ahead of me, by parcel service, went cartons of stuff—fabric and batting for my quilt. I was carrying the precious beads with me. I had dusted the dollhouse and set it in order the night before. Since I was departing on Sunday, Miss Edna was in her shiny best black, just as she had been when I first met her.

"It's my hope that you will come back after the summer," she said, "and that I will be alive and well, and ready to start a new quilt. I'm thinking of doing a Rose of Sharon like the one I told you about that I had as a child. You can come back and help me and learn some more."

"Yes," I said, hugging her. "I will."

"Happy graduation to you, Amy. I've a gift for you, but it's for the future. You will have the dollhouse after me, if you like, because I can see that you love it and will care for it, and hand it on to some other children one day. It is meant for children, after all."

"Oh!" I said, "*if* I like!" It was all I could say.

"Yes, I want you to have it." She brushed tears from those lovely white eyelashes. "And tell your mother to wear sensible shoes. And if she's smart, she'll marry Jim because then she'll get the Double Wedding Ring—after the Fair, of course. So, when you've finished your Bennington Stitch quilt she'll have two fine covers. A solid way to start a marriage, even a late marriage. Quilts make for a warm household."

Once again I hugged her, and then I left without looking back—so sure was I that I would be returning very soon.

22

"All right, ready? 'I never met an ape I didn't like.' "

Since Mom avoided 'trashy' movies, *she* didn't know. But I knew. *"Planet of the Apes,"* I said.

Mr. O nodded. "Doris, another of the same genre. 'What put the ape in apricot?' "

He had walked us home after Senior Night, two hours of student music including imitations: one of Mick Jagger doing "Jumping Jack Flash"; one of Michael Jackson's "Thriller"; and two of Elvis: "Hound Dog" and "Jailhouse Rock," done with a swiveling pelvis that made Mr. Rooter quickly swivel his head into his hands so he couldn't see. Mr. Rooter thinks the waltz is a suggestive dance.

I was not part of the musical program because I have a voice like a llama. Instead, I baked giant butterscotch cookies that sold for fifty cents each, proceeds to the Senior Class Gift. Every single cookie had sold, but I'd put away a half-dozen at home for us. We were in the kitchen now, having them with apple herb tea.

"Courage. The Cowardly Lion in *The Wizard of Oz*," Mom said.

"You are a very smart woman."

"Nonsense. You just need new material, Jim."

That didn't faze him. "The classics are eternally in order," he said pompously, in an exact imitation of Mr. McHugh, who teaches Greek Civilization. "The Cowardly Lion is an immortal."

"I agree," Mom said good-naturedly.

"I said you were smart. I just wonder if you're smart enough—and if you have enough courage."

"For what?" she wondered. "Smart and courageous enough for what?"

"To go to Bennington College and get yourself a degree," he said nonchalantly, biting into a cookie.

Unfortunately, Mom had just taken a sip of hot tea. She began to cough and sputter, but waved away our offers to paddle her on the back. "Bennington?" she gasped at last. "Bennington?"

"Yes, you know the place. Small college. Southern Vermont. Artsy."

"Jim!" Her voice was small but commanding.

"Listen. And Amy, you listen carefully too because you'll have to give your consent. Bennington has just started offering a Master of Fine Arts program in Creative Writing."

"But I can't go away to college. I'm a middle-aged woman who lives and works in Connecticut. I haven't the money. And then there's Amy to consider."

128

"Amy's going to be away quilting for a while. And *you* don't have to go anywhere. It's a non-resident degree they're offering."

Mom's eyes were huge, luminous green in her pale face. She looked absolutely lovely.

"Eventually you would have to spend a little time on their campus, but you'd want to. You've spent your life wanting to. They only require two one-month sessions and a one-week tutorial residency. But not at the beginning. Later on." He dug a brochure out of his jacket's inner pocket. "This came in this morning's mail and the minute I saw it I said to myself, *I know the perfect person, the absolutely perfect person for this program.*"

Mom took the announcement and began to pore over it, slowly, slowly, so as not to miss anything. "Listen," she said, and read from it. " 'A finished manuscript—a collection of short stories, or poems, or a novel, etc.—must be submitted for the degree.' "

"I noted that," Mr. O said. "You probably have enough manuscripts in your attic now for three degrees."

"I think I would try to do a complete final draft of my novel, at last," Mom said.

"Go for it, Mom." I was very excited. "Go for it!"

Mom looked dazed. "Jim, do you really think they'd have me?"

"They'd be crazy not to. You're already such a fine writer. They'll just get the credit for teaching you."

"Yes, I'd do the novel," Mom said. "I would do it. Finally."

129

"Why don't you phone them tomorrow and get the details?" Mr. O suggested. "There's probably a lot more information to be had."

I left them there in the kitchen talking in that happy, animated way. I had not seen my mother quite so excited about anything for years and years. I went to bed. Two hours later, I got up to go to the bathroom and I heard them still down there in the kitchen. I heard Mom's voice going steadily. She was reading from her novel, reading it aloud to someone, at last.

She did phone Bennington next morning, and they sent a pile of materials, including sample reading lists that would weary a genius. But Mom had read most of the stuff many times, and she loved it all.

The day before my graduation she got a big fat letter. She was in!

Graduation was very sweet and excruciatingly boring. Mr. Rooter talked forever about the *real world* out there that we were entering. If he thinks high school, and SATs, and gym classes, and adolescence, and all we'd lived through is not real and harsh, he is way out of touch. Life couldn't be much harder. However, we were getting older and maybe we'd be better able to cope.

Mr. McHugh recited the Ephebic Oath in Greek—at least that was what he said it was—and then we sang "Land of Hope and Glory" and our school song, "Bright Eastfield Banners"; that made my eyes tear a lot. Then it was over.

I had to say good-bye to Rob, who was going back that night to the hospital he'd done his project in, to work there for the summer, this time as a paid assistant in art therapy. In the fall he would be at SUNY Purchase, a Fine Arts major. His mother and his brother Pete were at graduation; his father was at a medical convention in Los Angeles.

We promised to write to one another, and when he got the

chance over the summer he'd come back to Eastfield to visit. And next year I'd be at Miss Edna's and he wouldn't be all that far away. "See you, Amy," he said, and I knew he would. I also knew that he was sad that his father had missed graduation. It couldn't be helped.

Jan's father and mother were both there, a united front. Her father seems nice (scruffy-looking with round shoulders; not nearly as handsome as Uncle George). The cram course had helped her get into Boston University, her *first* choice. "I won't say good-bye," she told me, "because I know you'll come up to Boston to see me. And I am definitely coming to see that dollhouse."

We didn't hang around and talk much afterward, or there would have been a lot of sadness at parting.

Mr. O gave me a lovely string of small pearls that had been his mother's. "Aunt Edna's suggestion," he said. "She has very good ideas." The pearls had an intricate gold clasp, very old and like nothing I ever saw before. I thought I'd like to wear the clasp in front. He also gave Mom a present for being mother of the graduate: a navy sweatshirt that said BENNINGTON in huge white letters.

I had baked a cake, a white butter-cream. I put two candles on it for good luck. After we cut the cake and ate it with the champagne Mr. O provided, Mom was a bit giddy. She was wearing flat Chinese slippers—at Miss Edna's advice—and she seemed very happy. "Jim," she began gratefully, "how can I ever thank you enough—" She stopped, stuck for the right words.

Mr. O, distinguished-looking in his light blue summer suit

with vest, seemed amazingly serious. "'A relationship is—is like a shark, you know. It has to constantly move forward or it dies. And I think what we got on our hands is a dead shark.'"

"Alvy Singer, that is, Woody Allen, in *Annie Hall*." I guessed, first shot, but they weren't listening to me.

Mom was looking at him intently. "Maybe the shark is not dead. Maybe it's just playing dead," she suggested softly.

"Doris, will you marry me?"

"Happy endings are so unfashionable," Mom murmured. "How will I be able to explain such a thing at Bennington? *Angst* is in."

SAT word! *Angst*: a feeling of anxiety.

"I'll go on movie binges periodically," Mr. O threatened, "and come home and tell you all the dreadful plots."

"In that case," Mom laughed, "yes. That qualifies as *angst* extraordinary."

"Hey, everybody," I announced, "you just won yourselves two patchwork quilts." Nobody paid me any attention. So I just went outside to sit on the back steps and admire myself in my yearbook picture.

In my opinion, happy endings may not be fashionable, but they are absolutely the best kind.